*Acting Edition*

I0589030

# Doctor Zhivago

Book by Michael Weller

Lyrics by Michael Korie &
Amy Powers

Music by Lucy Simon

Based on the novel by
Boris Pasternak

Produced with permission of Warner Bros.
Theatre Ventures, Inc. and Turner
Entertainment Co.

Orchestrations by Daniel Troob

Music Arrangements by Eric Stern

---

**FOR PRODUCTION INQUIRIES**

UNITED STATES AND CANADA
info@concordtheatricals.com
1-866-979-0447

UNITED KINGDOM AND EUROPE
licensing@concordtheatricals.co.uk
020-7054-7298

Each title is subject to availability from Concord Theatricals Corp.,
depending upon country of performance. Please be aware that
DOCTOR ZHIVAGO may not be licensed by Concord Theatricals Corp.
in your territory. Professional and amateur producers should contact
the nearest Concord Theatricals Corp. office or licensing partner to
verify availability.

---

No one shall make any changes in this title(s) for the purpose of production. No part of this book may be reproduced, stored in a retrieval system, scanned, uploaded, or transmitted in any form, by any means, now known or yet to be invented, including mechanical, electronic, digital, photocopying, recording, videotaping, or otherwise, without the prior written permission of the publisher. No one shall share this title(s), or any part of this title(s), through any social media or file hosting websites.

For all inquiries regarding motion picture, television, online/digital and other media rights, please contact Concord Theatricals Corp.

## THIRD-PARTY MATERIALS USE NOTE

Licensees are solely responsible for obtaining formal written permission from copyright owners to use copyrighted third-party materials (e.g., incidental music not provided in connection with a performance license, artworks, logos) in the performance of this play and are strongly cautioned to do so. If no such permission is obtained by the licensee, then the licensee must use only original materials and materials that the licensee owns and controls. Licensees are solely responsible and liable for clearances of all third-party copyrighted materials, and shall indemnify the copyright owners of the play(s) and their licensing agent, Concord Theatricals Corp., against any costs, expenses, losses and liabilities arising from the use of such copyrighted third-party materials by licensees. For music, please contact the appropriate music licensing authority in your territory for the rights to any incidental music not provided in connection with a performance license.

## IMPORTANT BILLING AND CREDIT REQUIREMENTS

If you have obtained performance rights to this title, please refer to your licensing agreement for important billing and credit requirements.

*DOCTOR ZHIVAGO* was first produced by Broadway Theatre in April 2015. Originally Produced on Broadway by Anita Waxman, Tom Dokton, Lattitude Link, Ted Hartley/RKO Stage and Chunsoo Shin with Margo & Roger Coleman, Corcoran Productions, J. Todd Harris, The Pelican Group, Chase Mishkin, Wasserman Shaw, Ahmos Hassan, Conrad Prebys & Debbie Turner, Adam Silberman, The Goldliner Group/Caroline Lieberman, Parrothead Productions, Bruce D. Long and La Jolla Playhouse.

Produced in association with Stage Entertainment, Broadway Across America, Grove Entertainment, The Shubert Organization, Tom McInerney, Joan & Irwin Jacobs, Susan Polis Schulz, Tilted Windmills, The Standford Group, Jim & Judy Harpel, John & Bonnie Hegeman Itai Shoffman & Sar Inbar, Dark Style Agency, Kelvingrove, Ventures, Stephanie Torreno/Eugenie & Keith Goggin, Rao Makineni/Jessica Green, David T. Loudermilk/Cheryl Lachowicz Robert & Debra Gottlieb/ Sharon Azrieli, Halloran Entertainment/LYUBOV Productions, Lois Weiner & Dr. Robert Weiner/Carl Pate, The Revolution Group/Samajaca Productions, Denise Rich and John Frost, Executive Producer, Junkyard Productions. The cast was as follows:

**PRIEST / KORNAKOV / ENSEMBLE** ...................Gary Milner

**ANNA GROMEKO** .........................Jacqueline Antaramian

**ALEXANDER GROMEKO** ...........................Jamie Jackson

**TONIA** ...........................................Lora Lee Gayer

**YOUNG TONIA** .................................. Ava-Riley Miles

**YURII ZHIVAGO** ....................................... Tam Mutu

**YOUNG YURII / SASHA** ...........................Jonah Halperin

**VIKTOR KOMAROVSKY**..............................Tom Hewitt

**MRS. GUISHAR / ENSEMBLE** ..................... Pilar Millhollen

**LARA GUISHAR**.................................... Kelli Barrett

**YOUNG LARA / KATARINA** .......................Sophia Gennusa

**PASHA ANTIPOV / STRELNIKOV**.............. Paul Alexander Nolan

**MARKEL / ENSEMBLE** ...................... Michael Brian Dunn

**NIKOLAI NIKOLAYOVICH / ENSEMBLE** .................Julian Cihi

**MISCHA / SHULYGIN / ENSEMBLE** .............. Joseph Medeiros

**ILYA / ENSEMBLE**................................. Spencer Moses

**TUSIA / SECRETARY OF TRIBUNAL / ENSEMBLE**.......Drew Foster

**GINTS / ENSEMBLE**............................ David McDonald

**LIBERIUS / ENSEMBLE** ........................... Josh Canfield

**YANKO / ENSEMBLE**............................... Robert Hager

**STEPKA /GOLYUBOVA / ENSEMBLE** ..............Wendi Bergamini

**OLYA / ENSEMBLE**...................... Briana Carlson-Goodman

**QUARTERMASTER / ENSEMBLE** . . . . . . . . . . . . . . . . . . . . . Bradley Dean

**KUBARIKHA / ENSEMBLE** . . . . . . . . . . . . . . . . . . . . . . . . . Melody Butiu

**YELENKA / ENSEMBLE** . . . . . . . . . . . . . . . . . . . . . . . . . . . Jesse Wildman

**ENSEMBLE** . . . . . . . . . . Heather Botts, Ericka Hunter, Julius Sermonia,

. . . . . . . . . . . . . . . . . . . . . . . . . . . . . . . . . . . . . . . . . . . . . . Jacob Smith

**SWINGS** . . . . . . . . . . . . . . . . . . . . . . . . Kira Guloien and Denis Lambert

**STANDBY** . . . . . . . . . . . . . . . Ashley Brooke (Young Yurii, Young Tonia,

. . . . . . . . . . . . . . . . . . . . . . . . . . . . . . Young Lara, Katarina, Sasha)

**UNDERSTUDIES** . . . . . . . . . . . . . . . Wendi Bergamini (Anna Gromeko),
Heather Botts (Lara Guishar, Tonia Gromeko), Josh Canfield
(Pasha Antipov/Strelnikov), Briana Carlson-Goodman (Lara
Guishar, Tonia Gromeko), Bradley Dean (Yurii Zhivago), Drew
Foster (Pasha Antipov/Strelnikov), David McDonald (Viktor
Komarovsky), and Gary Milner (Alexander Gromeko)

# CHARACTERS

## PRINCIPALS

**YURII ZHIVAGO** – A doctor and poet

**LARA GUISHAR** – Yurii's inspiration

**VIKTOR KOMAROVSKY** – A lawyer

**PASHA ANTIPOV/STRELNIKOV** – A revolutionary

**TONIA GROMEKO** – Yurii's wife

**ALEXANDER GROMEKO** – Tonia's father

**ANNA GROMEKO** – Tonia's mother

**SASHA** – Yurii and Tonia's son

## SUPPORTING

Liberius, Yanko, Kubarikha, Stepka/Golyubova, Shulygin, Yelenka, Markel, Young Tonia, Young Lara, Katarina, Young Yurii (also doubled as Sasha in the original production), Kubarikha, Olya, Nikolai, Tusia, Gints, Kornakov, Mischa, Mrs. Guishar.

## ENSEMBLE

The original Broadway production had a supporting and ensemble cast of 21: 10 women, 11 men.

With role-doubling and tripling, a flexible number of actors cover the roles of the above supporting characters, as well as Priest, Muscovites, Wedding Guests, Students, Cossacks, Soldiers, Nurses, Writer's Committee, Quartermaster, Women Field Workers, Partisans, Refugees, Bureaucrats, and Mourners.

# SETTING

Russia in the first decades of the twentieth century.

# MUSICAL NUMBERS

## Act One

1. "Two Worlds"................ Young Yurii, Yurii, Young Tonia, Tonia, Young Lara, Lara, Pasha, Priest, & Ensemble
1a. "Komarovsky's Toast"......Komarovsky, Tonia, Alex, Anna, & Guests
2. "Who Is She?"............................................ Yurii
2a. "The Tavern"..........................................Students
3. "It's A Godsend"............................... Pasha & Students
3a. "Godsend Exit".......................................Students
4. "When the Music Played"................................. Lara
04a. "Pasha's Exit" .......................................Orchestra
5. "Who Is She? (Reprise)"................................. Yurii
6. "Watch the Moon"...............................Yurii & Tonia
6a. "March Transition" .......................... Liberius & Soldiers
7. "Forward March for the Tsar" ................Gints, Soldiers, Pasha, Liberius & Yanko
7a. "Nurse Antipova".....................................Orchestra
7b. "Field Infirmary" ....................................Orchestra
8. "Home Where the Lilacs Grow" .................. Olya & Ensemble
9. "Forward March (Reprise)" ............................Orchestra
9a. "Yanko's Death" .....................................Orchestra
10. "Now"...............................................Yurii & Lara
11. "Blood on the Snow" ...... Gints, Pasha, Liberius, Soldiers & Nurses
12. "The Perfect World"................... Shulygin, Fetislova, Sasha, Komarovsky, & Ensemble
12a. "Komarovsky's Lament" .......................... Komarovsky
13. "Yurii's Decision" ...................................... Yurii
14. "In This House" ............. Sasha, Alex, Tonia, Yurii, & Ensemble

## Act Two

15. "Women and Little Children/He's There" ... Lara, Earthy Woman, & Female Ensemble
15a. "Arrival at Yuriatin" ..................................Orchestra
16. "No Mercy at All".................................... Strelnikov
16a. "No Mercy at All (Playoff)".........................Orchestra
16b. "Yelenka's Letter/In This House (Reprise)" ..................Alex

# ACT ONE

## Scene 1–1A: Gravesite in Moscow; 1903

### [MUSIC NO. 01 – TWO WORLDS]

*(A brief overture ends with the tolling of funeral bells.)*

### Projection title: CEMETARY OUTSIDE MOSCOW, 1903

*(A chorus of wealthy* **MUSCOVITES** *gathers in black fur-trimmed coats holding umbrellas, their* **SERVANTS** *beside them all dressed fashionably. An air of gloom prevails; it's the funeral of a suicide.)*

**MUSCOVITES.**
SVJATI BOŽE,
SVJATI KRJEPKI,
SVJATI BEZSMERTNI,
POMILUJ NAS.

EVER SINCE THE ANCIENT RIDERS
CROSSED THE GREAT DIVIDE,
RUSSIA IS A LAND WHERE
JOY AND SORROW COINCIDE.

TWO WORLDS, OF THE PLOUGH AND THE SWORD.
TWO WORLDS, OF THE SERF AND THE LORD.
TWO WORLDS, THE OPPRESSED, THE ELITE,
AND NEVER THE TWO SHALL MEET.

> *(The* **MUSCOVITES** *join a* **PRIEST** *who steps forward surrounded by the Gromeko family;* **ANNA, ALEX** *and their nine-year-old daughter* **TONIA** *facing a coffin where ten-year-old* **YURII ANDREYEVICH** *kneels. Also present;* **VIKTOR KOMAROVSKY**, *sleek and self-assured.)*

**KOMAROVSKY.** *(To the boy.)* Yurii Andreyevich Zhivago, say goodbye to your father...

> *(***YOUNG YURII** *kneels at the coffin.)*

**YOUNG YURII.**
> WHY HAVE YOU LEFT ME ALONE IN THE WORLD?
> WHAT DID I DO THAT WAS WRONG?
> PAPA, DON'T FLOAT AWAY
> LIKE A LEAF ON THE WIND.
> TELL ME WHERE I BELONG.

**MUSCOVITES.**
> TWO WORLDS, OF THE FLESH ON THE EARTH.
> TWO WORLDS, OF THE SOUL IN REBIRTH.
> TWO WORLDS, LIKE THE SMOKE FROM A FLAME
> WE RETURN FROM WHERE WE CAME.

**KOMAROVSKY.** Poor child, imagine being born a Zhivago – Zhivago factories, Zhivago estates... and suddenly it's gone; mother dead, now his father squanders the family fortune and jumps in front of a train.

**ALEX.** Viktor, as the father's lawyer you'll of course decide the boy's future, but our family has always been close –

**ANNA.** *(Chiming in, interrupting.)* – He can live with us, of course! Our little Tonia always dreamed of having a brother.

**KOMAROVSKY.**     Alexander Alexandrovich... Anna Ivanovna.

*(To the boy.)*

The Gromekos have offered you a home, Yurii Andreyevich.

**YOUNG YURII**. *(Fiercely.)* Get *away* from me!

**ANNA**. *(Gesturing to **TONIA**.)* Speak to him, Tonia.

**YOUNG TONIA**.  Come live with us, Yurii Andreyevich. We'll be best friends forever and ever.

> *(**YOUNG YURII** allows **YOUNG TONIA** to lead him off with the **GROMEKOS**, and **PRIEST**.)*

> *(As the family exits, **KOMAROVSKY** crosses to another part of the graveyard, a far less opulent grave attended by a weeping mother and her watchful young daughter.)*

> *(The **MUSCOVITES** remain.)*

## Scene 1–1B: Graveyard, Funeral of Lara's Father

### Projection Title: SIX MONTHS LATER

**MUSCOVITE WOMEN.**
SOME ARE BORN TO PRIVILEGE
AND FRIENDS WHO THEY CAN TRUST.

**MUSCOVITE MEN.**
SOME CONDEMNED TO POVERTY
WILL TURN TO WHOM THEY MUST.

**ALL.**
TWO WORLDS, ONE OF COMFORT AND EASE.
TWO WORLDS, ONE THAT SERVES ON ITS KNEES.
TWO WORLDS, OF THE WOLF AND HIS PREY,
AND THE WOLF ALWAYS GETS HIS WAY.

> (**MUSCOVITES** *exit.* **KOMAROVSKY** *comforts the bereaved widow,* **MRS. GUISHAR**.)

**KOMAROVSKY.**  We mourn your loss, Mrs. Guishar, but rest assured I'll take pains to see that your husband's finances are handled as he'd have wished.

**MRS. GUISHAR.**  *(Leaning weakly against him.)* How can I ever thank you, Counselor Komarovsky.

> (**KOMAROVSKY** *puts his other arm around* **YOUNG LARA**, *the child, as he steers them off and out of the cemetery.)*

## Scene 1–1C: Attic of Gromeko House

(**YOUNG TONIA** *leads a mystified* **YOUNG YURII** *into a cluttered space.*)

**YOUNG TONIA.** This is my secret room, no one else knows it's here.

**YOUNG YURII.** It's just an attic...

**YOUNG TONIA.** *(Giggling with delight.)* No, it's a castle, and up here I rule the whole house below.

**YOUNG YURII.** Am I the king, then?

**YOUNG TONIA.** When we're here you can be anything you want to be...!

## Scene 1–1D: The Dress Shop

(**YOUNG LARA**, **MRS. GUISHAR** *and* **KOMAROVSKY** *view a vacant shop.* **LARA**, *in school-girl uniform with high socks, studies a dressmaker's dummy.* **MRS. GUISHAR** *gazes around, overwhelmed.*)

**KOMAROVSKY**. I'll buy you the lease. With Lara's help – your daughter's a hard worker, I can see – the two of you could have great success with a dress shop like this.

**MRS. GUISHAR**. You've been such a comfort since my good husband died. If only I knew how to repay your kindness – Counselor Komarovsky.

**KOMAROVSKY**. 'Viktor,' please. Let me show you the private rooms above?

(*Turning to* **YOUNG LARA**.)

Pull your stocking up, Lara. It's distracting.

(*He leads* **MRS. GUISHAR** *upstairs.* **YOUNG LARA** *blushes, studies the mannequin.*)

## Scene 1–1E: Gromeko House

(**YOUNG TONIA** *hands* **YOUNG YURII** *a notebook.*)

**YOUNG TONIA.**
HERE IS A BOOK FOR YOUR THOUGHTS AND YOUR
DREAMS.

**YOUNG YURII.**
WHERE ARE THE WORDS?

**YOUNG TONIA.**
IN YOU.
SIMPLY WRITE FROM YOUR HEART,
THAT'S HOW ALL POETS START.
PUSHKIN WAS YOUNG ONCE, TOO.

## Scene 1–1F: The Dress Shop

*(**YOUNG LARA** doesn't see **KOMAROVSKY** watching her at the door as she confides to her dressmaker's mannequin.)*

**YOUNG LARA.**
SOMETIMES I FEEL SO ALONE IN THE WORLD.
WORK NEVER SEEMS TO END.
NOW THAT PAPA IS GONE
AND OUR OLD LIFE IS LOST,

*(To the mannequin.)*

YOU ARE MY ONLY FRIEND.

**KOMAROVSKY.**  Wouldn't you like to have a dress of your own just like that one day, and go dancing late into the night with someone?

*(**YOUNG LARA** makes a playful half-bow, and **KOMAROVSKY** exits with a wry flourish.)*

**YOUNG YURII.**
I WATCH THE RISING MOON APPEAR,
AND I CAN HEAR THE WORDS WITHIN ME.
HERE IN THE NIGHT,
ALL OF MOSCOW IN SIGHT,
WHAT WILL MY FUTURE BE?

*(The 'child characters' are joined by adult versions of each. **TONIA** a well-dressed young lady; **LARA** a sexually precocious sixteen-year old school girl, **YURII** a serious young medical school graduate.)*

**YOUNG TONIA.**        **YOUNG LARA.**    **YOUNG YURII.**
    WHAT WILL MY
       FUTURE BE?       WHAT WILL MY
          FUTURE BE?        WHAT WILL MY
             FUTURE BE?

**TONIA.**
    WHAT WILL MY
    FUTURE        **LARA.**          **YURII.**
       BE?       WHAT WILL IT
          BE?          WHAT WILL MY
             FUTURE BE?

## Scene 1–1G: Gromeko House

### Projection Title: AUGUST 1914

*(Now grown,* **TONIA** *stands beside grown* **YURII** *holding a framed diploma.)*

**TONIA.** 'Yurii Andreyevich Zhivago, Doctor of Medicine.'

**YURII.** Thanks to everything your family's done for me.
HOW CAN I EVER EXPRESS WHAT I FEEL,
MY SENSE OF IMMENSE SATISFACTION.
A USEFUL CAREER, A LICENSE TO HEAL,
A WAY TO REPAY WHAT I'VE BEEN GIVEN.

*(Takes* **TONIA***'s hand in his.)*

SOON TO WED MY DEAREST FRIEND,
FINDING MY ROLE, PURPOSE, AND GOAL.

**TONIA.**
THAT'S WHAT OUR LIVES ARE FOR.

**BOTH.**
HOW COULD WE ASK FOR MORE?

*(***TONIA** *folds herself into his arms.)*

## Scene 1–1H: The Dress Shop

> (**PASHA** *enters with urgency, carrying a bundle.*)

**PASHA.** The protest is on for tonight. We're blocking the tracks. The Tsar won't be able to move any troops to the front.

**LARA.** *(Takes out a wrapped bundle.)* Here, the pamphlets are ready... I had them printed on the dress shop account.

**PASHA.** High fashion paying for the war against German fascists; perfect!

**LARA.** Leave the gun here, Pasha; you can't be caught with a weapon.

**PASHA.** *(Handing it to her with bravado.)* If you hear I've been arrested, throw it in the river.

**LARA.** Please don't take chances, Pasha...

> (**PASHA** *pecks* **LARA** *on the cheek.*)

**PASHA.** *(Flirtatious high spirits.)* Never worry about Pasha Antipov; I'm a cat: nine lives.

> (**PASHA** *exits quickly as* **LARA** *conceals the gun in the clothing on the dress mannequin.*)

## Scene 1–1l: Street past the Gromeko House

(**STUDENTS** *with banners demonstrate against the Tsar's war with Germany.*)

**STUDENTS.**
RUSSIA ARISE!
JOIN IN THE RALLY!
SPEAK OUT,
AND LET YOUR VOICE BE HEARD!

(**PASHA** *enters and distributes pamphlets.*)

**PASHA.**
LET YOUR VOICE BE HEARD!
FLOOD EV'RY STREET!
FILL EV'RY ALLEY!
STAND TALL,

**STUDENTS.**
STAND TALL!

**PASHA.**
AND HELP US

**PASHA & STUDENTS.**
SPREAD THE WORD!
END THE WAR, AND FEED THE PEOPLE!

**PASHA.**
TAKE CONTROL, AND OVERTHROW...

**PASHA & STUDENTS.**
TWO WORLDS!

(*A burst of loud gunfire.* **THREE COSSACKS** *enter, breaking up the student protest.*)

## Scene 1–1J: Balcony of Gromeko House

(**YURII** *watches* **TWO COSSACKS** *pursue one of the* **STUDENTS**. *Distant gunfire.* **TONIA** *hurries out onto the balcony to* **YURII**.)

**TONIA**. You have to finish dressing, darling, you can't be late for your own wedding!

**YURII**. They've sent Cossacks to clear the railway tracks. They'll need a doctor if there's trouble.

(**MARKEL**, *an old family servant, bustles out onto the balcony worried.*)

**MARKEL**. You mustn't be out here young master, the streets are dangerous.

**YURII**. Bring my bag, Markel. They'll need help at the rail yard...

**TONIA**. Yurii, no! The ceremony's in less than an hour.

(*But* **YURII** *is already gone.*)

## Scene 1–1K: The Dress Shop

(**KOMAROVSKY** *approaches* **LARA** *from behind and kisses her neck.*)

**LARA**. Viktor, I told you never to come here again. No, Vikor, I can't do this anymore.

**KOMAROVSKY**. *(Clasps her breasts, pulls her close.)* Why not? Is your student agitator friend putting subversive ideas in your head?

*(She doesn't answer.)*

Does the little Marxist know how to satisfy you like I do?

*(She tries to slap him. He grabs her wrist. She holds herself at a distance. He kisses her passionately.)*

**LARA**. No Viktor; please stop. Please, don't come here again.

**KOMAROVSKY**. I'll return at midnight If you're gone, I might have to find your radical friend and describe things I taught you that would make even a professional lady blush.

*(**KOMAROVSKY** leaves. **LARA**, unsettled and full of mounting panic and fear takes **PASHA**'s gun from inside the tailor's dummy, grabs her coat, tucks the revolver up the hollow of her muff and races into the street.)*

## Scene 1–1L: The Street outside the Gromekos

(**YURII** *rushes into streets alive with riot and gunfire.* **MARKEL** *hands him his medical bag as* **COSSACKS** *chase a* **PROTESTER** *on.*)

(**PASHA** *enters helping an* **INJURED COMRADE** *and spots* **YURII** *with his medical bag.*)

**PASHA.** Can you stitch him up, Doctor?

(**PASHA** *races off.* **YURII** *examines the injured* **COMRADE***.*)

**YURII.** Head wounds look worse than they are, you'll be fine.

(**KOMAROVSKY** *crosses to the cathedral where the wedding will take place. He is dressed for the ceremony ahead.*)

**KOMAROVSKY.** Get back inside, Zhivago. Cossacks are firing on the crowd.

(**KOMAROVSKY** *hurries to the cathedral. More gunfire.*)

**YURII.** Luckily you were only grazed.

(**LARA**, *pursuing* **KOMAROVSKY**, *passes* **YURII**. **YURII** *turns back to his house. They cross paths, each in their own world, but their pace may slow briefly – unconscious magnetism.*)

(**MARKEL** *takes* **YURII**'s *medical bag as wedding guests begins to assemble. At the last moment* **YURII** *runs on for this wedding.*)

## Scene 1–1M: Russian Orthodox Cathedral

(**GUESTS** *form the aisle of the wedding procession.*)

(**YURII**, *his publisher friend* **NIKOLAI**, *and a* **MATRON** *of honor stand at the altar with a Russian Orthodox* **PRIEST**. **ALEX** *and* **ANNA** *lead the veiled* **TONIA** *down the aisle to the altar.*)

**ENSEMBLE.**
AH, AH

**PRIEST.**
HAVE YOU, YURII ANDREYOVICH,
PROMISED YOURSELF TO ANY OTHER WOMAN?

**YURII.**
I AM PROMISED TO HER ALONE, FATHER.

**ENSEMBLE.**
AH, AH

**PRIEST.**
HAVE YOU, ATONINA ALEXANDROYNA,
PROMISED YOURSELF TO ANY OTHER MAN?

**TONIA.**
I AM PROMISED TO HIM ALONE, FATHER.

**PRIEST.**
BLESSED SHALL YOU BE AS HUSBAND AND WIFE.

(**YURII** *puts a ring on* **TONIA**'s *finger.*)

**ENSEMBLE.**
AH, AH, AH
TWO HEARTS, OF A HUSBAND AND WIFE.
TWO RINGS, IN THE UNION OF LIFE.
TWO SOULS, INTERTWINED INTO ONE.
IN THE EYES OF THE HEAVENLY FATHER AND SON.

*(The* **PRIEST** *lights the couple's candles.)*

**ALL.**

AND WE CROWN THEM WITH GLORY AND HONOR!

*(Transition:* **GUESTS** *begin to turn from the wedding and face forward to suggest a new locale.)*

**GUESTS.**

TWO WORLDS! AS IT EVER HAS BEEN.
TWO WORLDS! EVER FASTER THEY SPIN.
CAUGHT IN THE TIDE.
PASSION AND PRIDE.
WHO CAN PREDICT WHAT THE FATES WILL DECIDE
WHEN TWO WORLDS COLLIDE!

*(A brilliant chandelier alights.)*

*(The cathedral has transitioned to...)*

## Scene 1–2: Grand Room in the Gromeko Home

**ALEX**. Family, friends, well-wishers...

### [MUSIC NO. 01A – KOMAROVSKY'S TOAST]

What a blessing on this night, with our streets in turmoil, and the Kaiser's army threatening our borders –

**ANNA**. Welcome to our home, welcome everyone.

**ALEX**. Yes, we thank you all for helping us celebrate tonight's –

**ANNA**. *(Interrupts.)* My two little playmates are husband and wife at last!

**ALEX**. *(Fondly.)* Thank you dear.

**ANNA**. *(Interrupting.)* – Could there be any better proof that all the cherished values of our world will endure through all time. Two great families united in marriage; Gromeko-Zhivago.

**ALEX**. And now if I may –

**ANNA**. *(Interrupting.)* Our beloved daughter Tonia – and a son of our very own...

*(Teary.)*

A *doctor!* Doctor Zhivago!

**NIKOLAI**. *(Steps forward unexpectedly.)* Doctor and poet. Yes, the next issue of our literary quarterly includes a poem by my friend and fellow versifier, Y.A. Zhivago.

**TONIA**. *(Surprised, to **YURII**.)* Is it true?

**YURII**. *(Embarrassed but proud.)* I thought we agreed not to speak a word of it, Nikolai Nikolayovich.

*(Polite laughter and applause from the* **GUESTS.***)*

**ALEX**. And now I call on Moscow's esteemed Counsellor at Law and our dear friend to toast this joyous union as only he knows how –

**ANNA**.  *(Again interrupting.)* Viktor Ippolitovich Komarovsky!

**ALEX**. Viktor, please.

**KOMAROVSKY**.
LOVELY LITTLE TONIA.
HAVEN'T YOU DONE WELL.
MARRYING THIS DOCTOR.

**TONIA**. *(Spoken in rhythm.)*
AND A POET!

**KOMAROVSKY**.
TIME WILL TELL.
TO MARRIAGE, AND CHILDREN!
THOSE BUSY BIRDS AND BEES.
MAY THE ANGELS BLESS YOUR HAPPINESS
AND SPARE ME FROM IT, PLEASE!

*(All laugh. He lifts his glass.)*

ZA VAS!

**GUESTS**.
TO YOU!

**KOMAROVSKY**.
AND A BOND THAT'S EVER TRUE.
LUBOV!

**GUESTS**.
TO LOVE!

**KOMAROVSKY**.
WHICH A MAN CAN NEVER HAVE TOO MUCH OF.

**ALEX.**
ZA VAS!

**GUESTS.**
TO LIFE!

**ANNA.**
LUBOV!

**GUESTS.**
TO LOVE!

**ALEX.**
CARRY ON OUR CUSTOMS.

**ANNA.**
CIVIL AND DISCREET.

**KOMAROVSKY.**
SO UNLIKE THE RABBLE
WREAKING HAVOC IN THE STREET.
REMEMBER, DEAR CHILDREN,
AS DOWN THE PATH YOU START:
THE ONLY REVOLUTION
IS THE ONE INSIDE YOUR HEART.

**GUESTS.**  Ah!

**KOMAROVSKY.**  And now, if our happy couple will lead us in the waltz!

> (*A formal dance.* **TONIA** *and* **YURII** *bow and come together arm in arm.* **GUESTS** *watch approvingly; the perfect Moscow marriage.* **KOMAROVSKY** *retires to a game of cards in the corner.* **GUESTS** *are soon all dancing; a stately rejoinder to the chaos outside.*)

> (**LARA GUISHAR** *enters in a thick overcoat and searches the room, approaches a* **YOUNG RAKE**.)

**LARA.** Where will I find Viktor Komarovsky?

**YOUNG RAKE.** In the corner, playing cards with Prosecutor Kornakov –

**LARA.** *(Abruptly.)* Dance with me.

> (**LARA** *dances him towards* **KOMAROVSKY** *playing cards with* **MOSCOW GRANDEES.**)

**YOUNG RAKE.** I don't think we've met before. How do you know Counselor Komarovsky?

> (**LARA** *dances the* **YOUNG RAKE** *to a position opposite* **KOMAROVSKY.**)

**LARA.** I should have done this long ago.

> (**KOMAROVSKY** *turns as she pulls* **PASHA***'s revolver from her muff and fires. A* **MAN** *beside* **KOMAROVSKY** *grabs his hand in pain. Momentary shock, then pandemonium erupts.*)
>
> (*Ad-lib, screams and shouts of panic from the crowd.*)

**KORNAKOV.** *(Wounded man.)* Assassin!! Someone stop her!!

> (**LARA***'s legs give way and she sinks to the floor.*)
>
> (**YURII** *rushes to her side, but* **KOMAROVSKY** *blocks his way.*)

**KOMAROVSKY.** Stay calm everyone, please, there's no danger; it was an accident.

> (*Ad lib, shouts of panic from the crowd.*)
>
> (**LARA** *recovers.*)

**KORNAKOV.**  Call the police, arrest that woman!!

**KOMAROVSKY.**  No!

*(To others.)*

Tell the musicians to keep playing.

*(Urgently instructing nearby men.)*

Take her into the conservatory. We need a doctor for prosecutor Kornakov.

*(***TWO MEN*** *take ***LARA*** *out.)*

## Scene 1–2B: Gromeko Conservatory

(**YURII** *leads* **KORNAKOV** *to an alcove where he stores his medical bag. While tending* **KORNAKOV***'s wound,* **YURII** *watches* **LARA** *through an open door to the Ballroom.*)

**KORNAKOV**. These revolutionists only know one answer to every problem: BANG!!! 'You don't like my politics; BANG.' 'You don't like my boots; BANG! Problem solved!'

## [MUSIC NO. 02 – WHO IS SHE?]

**YURII**. She doesn't look like a radical to me.

**KORNAKOV**. They're ALL radicals at the University. I say graduate 'em with a taste of their own medicine – 'Here's your diploma; congratulations, BANG!'

(**YURII**, *mesmerized by* **LARA** *as he bandages* **KORNAKOV**, *sees her led from the main hall.*)

**YURII**.
A GIRL WALKS IN, SHE SHOOTS A GUN.
WHO IS SHE?
SHE DOESN'T CRY, SHE DOESN'T RUN.
WHO IS SHE?
WHAT CLOUDS HER PRETTY FACE WITH HATE?
WHAT BROUGHT HER TO THIS FEVERED STATE
TO SHOOT A ROYAL MAGISTRATE?
WHO IS SHE?

(**KOMAROVSKY** *crosses to the* **TWO MEN** *who have* **LARA** *between them.* **KORNAKOV** *joins them.*)

**KOMAROVSKY**. I'll handle this. We don't want to embarrass our hosts with a scandal.

*(The* **TWO MEN** *exit, leaving* **KOMAROVSKY**
*alone with* **LARA**.*)*

You damn fool, you know what you just did?

**LARA.**  I shot the wrong man.

**KOMAROVSKY.**  Enough childish drama, Lara. We'll meet
at the dress shop at midnight and talk it over –

**LARA.**  Come near me and I'll shoot you again – only next
time my hand won't shake.

*(A standoff.* **YURII***, tying* **KORNAKOV**'*s
bandage, can't hear their argument.)*

**YURII.**

SHE SEEMS TO KNOW HIM FAR TOO WELL …
WHY WOULD SHE?
AS IF SHE HOLDS HIM IN SOME SPELL …
WHY SHOULD SHE?
TOO YOUNG TO NEED A MAN LIKE THAT,
A CRASS, CONNIVING BUREAUCRAT
UNLESS… IS THIS A LOVER'S SPAT?
HOW COULD SHE?

**KOMAROVSKY.**  *(Amused.)* Ungrateful child. I should have
been satisfied with your mother.

*(***LARA** *spits at his feet and starts off.)*

**YURII.**

THE BLAZE IN HER EYES …
A STORM ON THE RISE,
DEFIANT AND DARING!
HOW WONDROUS THE THRILL
TO FOLLOW YOUR WILL
WITHOUT EVEN CARING …

*(**LARA** rushes in looking for an exit and encounters **YURII** packing his supplies. She hesitates.)*

How do you know Viktor Komarovsky?

**LARA**. *(Impulsively.)* For your own sake, doctor, stay out of this.

*(**LARA** breaks free of **YURII**'s gaze and runs out. **YURII** is baffled.)*

**YURII**.
A CRIMINAL EVADES ARREST.
HOW DOES SHE?
SHE FLEES THE SCENE
AND NONE PROTEST.
WHO WAS SHE?
THE ORCHESTRA RESUMES THE BEAT.
THE SERVANTS POUR CHATEAU LAFITE.
SHE FADES INTO A WINTER STREET,
AND NO ONE SEEMS TO CARE.
WHO IS SHE?
WAS SHE EVER THERE?

**KOMAROVSKY**. *(Rushing in.)* Lara!

**YURII**. *(Confronts him.)* It was you she meant to shoot, wasn't it!?

**KOMAROVSKY**. Young Zhivago, you've enjoyed a fine start in society: doctor; poet, so they say; bravo! Who knows, you may one day even restore the luster to the name your father tarnished. But a word of advice. Never pry into another gentleman's private business.

**YURII**. Did you pay for this 'private business' with my father's money?

**KOMAROVSKY**. *(A dark look.)* Careful, Zhivago. I can be a valuable friend to have... but a much more dangerous enemy.

> *(With winning camaraderie.)*

Come, they'll miss us.

> *(**KOMAROVSKY** exits.)*

> *(**YURII** remains, following the path **LARA** took outside to...)*

## Scene 1–2C: The Street

*(Following her, **YURII** hurries outside and looks for which direction **LARA** went.)*

YURII.
THE BRANCHES OF THE MOONLIT TREES
CONCEAL HER.
YET SOMEHOW IN A SUDDEN BREEZE
I FEEL HER ...
THAT TOUCH OF DANGER IN THE AIR
INVISIBLE BUT EV'RYWHERE,
THEN GONE THE MOMENT THAT IT'S THERE,

*(**YURII** sees **LARA** hurrying away, huddled in her coat. He watches her pass.)*

A SHADOW ON THE SNOW ...

*(**LARA** vanishes.)*

THE DRAMA HAS PASSED.
IT'S QUIET AT LAST.
NO STORM IN THE MAKING.
SO WHY DO I STAND
STILL CLENCHING MY HANDS
TO STOP THEM FROM SHAKING?
WHO IS SHE? WHO IS SHE?

*(He watches the dark street where she disappeared. **TONIA** appears behind him from the conservatory.)*

TONIA. Yurii? Come inside, we're all waiting.

*(She returns inside.)*

YURII.
WHO IS SHE ...?

(**YURII** *watches* **LARA** *disappear into the night, then follows* **TONIA** *inside.*)

(*Across the stage a noisy cheer erupts as the scene transitions to...*)

## Scene 1–3: Tavern in the Student Quarter

### Projection Title: A FEW WEEKS LATER

### [MUSIC NO. 02A – THE TAVERN]

(**STUDENTS** *carry* **PASHA** *in for a celebration, as they mock-march.* **TUSIA** *leaps on a bench.*)

**STUDENTS.**
HOY! HOY! HOY! HOY!
HOY! HOY! HOY! HOY!
HOY! HOY! HOY! HOY!
HOY! HOY! HOY! HOY!
HOY! HOY! HOY!

**TUSIA.** *(Expansively.)* A toast. May 'Pasha the Cat' return from this war with ALL nine lives untouched...

**ILYA.** *(Over the cheering.)* ...and for each of his lives may he leave ten dead Germans behind.

*(They all raise glasses and toast loudly.)*

**PASHA.** *(Leaping up beside* **ILYA**.*)* Ilya, I didn't volunteer so I could kill Germans. I'm going to the front to recruit the recruits; teach them to aim their weapons at the true enemy: our incompetent, pathetic Tsar!

*(All agree with gusto.* **LARA** *steps forward.)*

**LARA.** I want to make a toast – while some of us are still sober enough to hear.

*(Facing* **PASHA**.*)*

Pasha jokes about enlisting but we know the dangers he'll face. Tonight we're here to wish him a safe return, but more than that, we celebrate a new beginning for Russia.

*(With a meaningful glance towards* **PASHA**.*)*

To new beginnings!

*(A* **STUDENT GUARD** *sees a* **COSSACK OFFICER** *pass in the street and whistles a sharp warning.* **LARA** *stops mid-sentence.)*

*(The* **COSSACK** *eyes* **STUDENTS** *inside and enters the tavern to 'investigate.' The room falls silent, tense.* **PASHA** *offers him vodka.)*

**PASHA**.  To the Motherland. Za vas!

*(The* **COSSACK** *drinks, nods, returns the bottles to* **PASHA** *and leaves. A moment of relief. The celebration resumes.)*

**MISCHA**.  I have a gift for the departing hero!

*(***STUDENTS** *press forward with gifts.)*

**ILYA**.  So do I! Pashenka, you're about to spend long winter nights in the trenches wondering why you ever left your friends behind, so here's something to remember us by...

*(He hands* **PASHA** *a large book.)*

**LARA**.  'Great Palaces of Russia.'

**PASHA**.  *(Joking disbelief.)* 'Great Palaces?' For a revolutionist?

*(Wryly.)*

Is this a joke, Ilya? What am I supposed to do with this on the front lines?

## [MUSIC NO. 03 - IT'S A GODSEND]

**ILYA**.  No, it's serious, it's, it's –

**PASHA**.  Of course, Ilya. I see now...

IT'S A BRILLIANT GIFT, YOUR RESILIENT GIFT
FOR THE RUSSIAN-GERMAN LINE,
FOR I CANNOT THINK OF ANY BETTER BULLET SHIELD
AS I DODGE AN EXPLODING MINE ...

*(He flips through the picture book's pages.)*

THAN A FAT BOOK OF PALACE PROTOCOL.
THE TSAR IN HIS MARBLE BILLIARD HALL.
MAY IT GUARD MY HEART AS MY COMRADES FALL
FROM SHRAPNEL OVERHEAD.
AND IF I'M HIT, WHO GIVES A SHIT?
LET THE TSAR TAKE ONE INSTEAD!

**STUDENTS.** Hoorah!

**PASHA.**
NO ORDINARY GIFT WE RECEIVE HERE!
IT'S A GODSEND!

**STUDENTS.**
IT'S A GODSEND!

**PASHA.**
TO REMIND US OF THE DECADENCE I LEAVE HERE,
IT'S A GODSEND!

**STUDENTS.**
TO A MARXIST END!

**PASHA.**
WHEN WE'RE SHIV'RING IN THE COLD
WITH OUR BODIES TURNING BLUE
AND THE FIRE IS DWINDLING
AND WE'RE LOW ON KINDLING
WHEN WE NEED TO LIGHT THE STOVE TO COOK,
IT'S A GODSEND – THIS BOOK!

**STUDENTS.** Gifts! Gifts! More gifts!

*(**MISCHA** steps forward, hands **PASHA** a gift wrapped in plain brown paper.)*

**MISCHA.** I found this in the marketplace.

    (**PASHA** *rips it open and out spills a woman's nightgown trimmed with lace.*)

**PASHA.** A woman's nightgown? For the front?

**MISCHA.** No, the clerk assured me it's a night-<u>*shirt*</u>, for a soldier!

**PASHA.** (*Looking at a tag inside it.*) Did you read inside, Mischa? 'Madelaine Vionnet, Paris, femmes, petite.' This must be for the French Army.

    (*Everyone laughs, catcalls, whistles, as* **PASHA** *holds the nightgown up against himself, facetiously.*)

SUCH A FESTIVE GIFT, THIS "SUGGESTIVE" GIFT
ALL MY TRENCH-MATES WILL REJOICE.
WHEN WE'RE DOUBLED UP IN SLEEPING BAGS
FOR WARMTH AT NIGHT,
I'LL BE EV'RYONE'S FIRST CHOICE!

    (**STUDENTS**' *raucous laughter. With a private look* **PASHA** *tosses the nightgown to* **LARA**, *who for some reason seems more than casually interested.*)

**STUDENTS.**
NO ORDINARY GIFT YOU IMPART HERE!

**PASHA.**
IT'S A GODSEND!

**STUDENTS.**
IT'S A GODSEND!

**PASHA.**
SPREAD *DAS KAPITAL* IN EVERY RUSSIAN HEART HERE,
FOR WE <u>START</u> HERE, MY SUBVERSIVE FRIENDS!

**ALL**.
> DA!

> (**PASHA** *and* **TUSIA** *dance the classic Cossack*
> *Barnya.* **TUSIA** *loses and* **PASHA** *triumphs.*)

**TUSIA**. So he dances well, I concede. You know what they say? Good dancer, bad lover.

**TUSIA'S FIANCÉE**. Or in your case, bad at both.

**TUSIA**. *(On his knees, to* **LARA**.) Beautiful Larissa, Pasha Antipov will never make you happy. Before it's too late, marry me.

**LARA**. Tusia... it's already too late.

> (*All respond with puzzled looks. She extends*
> *her hand to* **PASHA**, *who comes forward.*)

**PASHA**. We're married.

> (*All stand in astonished silence.*)

**VARIOUS**. How could you not tell us? Married? Is it true? When did this happen?

**LARA**. This morning I became Larissa Antipova...

**PASHA**. What German would dare take my life, when Lara's waiting for me in Moscow.

> (**PASHA** *lifts* **LARA** *onto a bench for all to see.*)

> IF INDEED THERE IS A GOD
> WHICH I'M NOT TOO CERTAIN OF,
> YOU'RE THE PROOF EMPIRICAL,
> A MODERN MIRACLE.

**PASHA & STUDENTS**.
> THE STARS SMILE DOWN
> FROM HEAVEN ABOVE...

**STUDENTS.**
FOR THE GODSEND IS LOVE!

### [MUSIC NO. 03A – GODSEND EXIT]

*(The* **STUDENTS** *lift* **LARA***'s bench, chanting.)*

HOY! HOY! HOY! HOY!
HOY! HOY! HOY! HOY!
HOY! HOY! HOY! HOY!

*(The procession of* **STUDENTS** *following* **PASHA** *and* **LARA** *into the night continues to circle silently as, simultaneously, lights rise elsewhere on...)*

## Scene 1–3B: Room in the Gromeko House

*(**YURII**, now in military uniform, searches for his notebook in his desk.)*

*(**MARKEL** meets him.)*

**MARKEL.** Hurry, young master, they're boarding your division. You mustn't miss the train.

**YURII.** Wait here. I won't be long.

**MARKEL.** But sir, if you're left behind you'll be disgraced.

**YURII.** Nothing else matters if I don't do this first.

*(Loud thunderclap; **MARKEL** hands him an umbrella as music grows agitated.)*

**MARKEL.** Here.

*(**YURII** heads out to the streets.)*

*(The procession of **STUDENTS** have by now delivered **PASHA** and **LARA** to their room.)*

## Scene 1–4: Lara and Pasha's Room

*(A bed;* **LARA** *and* **PASHA** *prepare for their wedding night.)*

**LARA**. Oh, Pasha, I feel like finally my true life is beginning.

*(Watching him flirtatiously.)*

I hope you don't mind... I wore your nightgown.

**PASHA**. Before we start – there's something I have to tell you.

**LARA**. Yes, we'll be honest and open with each other always! No secrets, no games. Tell me.

**PASHA**. *(Suddenly awkward.)* Our friends expect me to always – I suppose they think – they think I know things, all *kinds* of things – it's true I'm very well educated. But in certain matters a man might be expected to know on his wedding night, I'm afraid I'm as innocent as you. Are you disappointed?

*(***LARA*** goes to him, troubled.)*

**LARA**. Pasha, please, just hold me.

**PASHA**. *(Confused, he holds her comfortingly.)* You're trembling, What is it?

**LARA**. How stupid to think I could wipe away the past by pretending it never happened.

**PASHA**. Nothing before tonight matters. We're making a new life together.

*(Flirtatious.)*

I'll always return to you on all four paws...

**LARA**. Listen to me, my love, and when I'm finished, if you've the smallest doubt that I'm the wife you need, promise you'll consider our marriage annulled.

**PASHA.** What kind of wild talk is this?

**LARA.** Shhhh, Pasha; promise.

**PASHA.** *(Worried pause.)* Very well.

**LARA.** That scandal,

### [MUSIC NO. 04 – WHEN THE MUSIC PLAYED]

the girl who shot the Chief Magistrate then vanished?

*(He waits for her to finish.)*

I never threw away your gun.

*(**PASHA** understands immediately.)*

I WAS YOUNG. I WAS POOR.
LIFE WAS HARSH AND UNSURE
BUT A FATHERLESS GIRL CAN'T COMPLAIN.
THEN MY FATE CHANGED BY CHANCE
WITH AN INNOCENT DANCE
WITH A MAN WHO WAS OLDER
AND RICHER AND BOLDER.
A MAN WITH A TASTE FOR CHAMPAGNE,
AND GIRLS LIKE ME,
TOO BLINDED TO SEE …
BUT WHEN THE MUSIC PLAYED
THE WORLD WOULD FADE AWAY.
AND I'D SAIL 'CROSS THE FLOOR,
CARING LESS, WANTING MORE.
WHEN THE MUSIC PLAYED,
SOMEHOW MY SOUL OBEYED.
HEAVEN WOULD BE WHISPERING MY NAME
WHEN THE MUSIC PLAYED.

*(Lights change. **KOMAROVSKY** appears, approaches the bed and sits beside **LARA**.)*

SO I GAVE AND HE TOOK.
WITH A WORD, WITH A LOOK,
I WAS CAPTURED INSIDE OF HIS GAME.
THERE I WAS STILL A GIRL
IN THE DEVIL'S OWN WORLD,
BUT A GIRL WHO WAS OLDER
AND WISER AND COLDER,
A GIRL WHO FELT HUNGER... AND SHAME.
YES, I SERVED LIKE A SLAVE.
SINS I'LL TAKE TO MY GRAVE...

(KOMAROVSKY and LARA dance.)

BUT WHEN THE MUSIC PLAYED
THE WORLD WOULD FADE AWAY,
AND I'D SAIL 'CROSS THE FLOOR
CARING LESS, WANTING MORE.
WHEN THE MUSIC PLAYED,
SOMEHOW MY SOUL OBEYED.
HEAVEN ONLY KNOWS WHAT I BECAME
WHEN THE MUSIC PLAYED.

(KOMAROVSKY leaves.)

AND I HATED HIM,
AND I WANTED HIM...
AND I MET WITH HIM MORE THAN I SHOULD.
AND IT FRIGHTENED ME,
HOW HE'D HOLD ME, LIKE HE OWNED ME.
I SAID: 'STAY AWAY,' BUT HE WOULDN'T.
OH GOD, 'STAY AWAY,' BUT I COULDN'T.
I HAD TO END IT, I HAD TO LIVE...
CAN YOU FORGIVE ME?
PUT THE PAIN ASIDE. PUT THE PAST AWAY.
LOOK INTO MY EYES...
AND LET THE MUSIC PLAY.
YESTERDAYS FADE AWAY
TO A WORLD WE RESTORE,

WANTING LESS, CARING MORE.
LET THE MUSIC PLAY
FOR WHO WE ARE TODAY.
LET ME HEAR YOU WHISPERING MY NAME
WHEN THE MUSIC PLAYS.
WHEN THE MUSIC PLAYS.
WHEN THE MUSIC PLAYS.

Pasha, I'm so sorry. Please say something? Am I forgiven?

**PASHA**.  *(Fighting tears of humiliation and rage.)* Forgiveness isn't enough for what that bourgeois bastard did to you!!

### [MUSIC NO. 04A – PASHA'S EXIT]

*(He dashes out. Frozen in shock for a moment,* **LARA** *finally runs to the door.)*

**LARA**.  Pasha!!

*(She races after him into the stormy night.)*

## Scene 1–4B: Street outside Lara's Rooming House

**LARA**. Pasha! Pashenka!!!

> *(Thunder. She wraps her coat tighter.* **YURII**, *in uniform, steps from the doorway holding an umbrella.)*

**YURII**. Do you by any chance remember me? The doctor, the night you shot the magistrate.

**LARA**. *(Very annoyed, trying to get past him.)* What are you *doing* here, what do you want!

**YURII**. *(Blurting disjointedly.)* Was it Viktor Komarovsky you meant to kill that night, I've wanted to ask you ever since!

**LARA**. *(Incredulous.)* You found out where I live?

**YURII**. Time is running out for me, I have to know before it's too late –

**LARA**. Are you *deranged*?! I have to find my husband!

### [MUSIC NO. 05 – WHO IS SHE? (REPRISE)]

> *(***YURII**, *at a loss, holds out his umbrella.)*

**YURII**. Please. *(Beat.)* Take this.

> *(***LARA**, *caught between fury and confusion snatches the umbrella and exits in a rush, turning back to look at him for the briefest moment. Yas underscoring starts,* **YURII** *thinks to himself, formulating the beginnings of a poem.)*

Husband...

A TOUCH OF DANGER IN THE AIR,
INVISIBLE BUT EV'RYWHERE ...

## Scene 1–5: The Train Station

*(MARKEL pulls a baggage hand-cart to YURII, waiting in his uniform. TONIA is right behind MARKEL. Behind her stands ALEX. ANNA bustles on with a small packet.)*

**ANNA.** Bring extra socks for the trenches. All that cold and damp are bad for your heart!

**YURII.** I'm carrying far too much already, Nana.

**TONIA.** Take the socks, Yurii.

**ALEX.** Always remember; we beat back Napoleon's army a hundred years ago. It cost millions of Russian lives, but the French learned a lesson, and the Germans will learn it all over again. The Tsar's armies are unconquerable. Our spirit is too strong...

**KOMAROVSKY.** *(Hurries on.)* Thank Heaven, I thought I'd miss you!

> *(Hands him a medal.)*

This Imperial Cross was presented to your father by the Tsar himself for valiant service in the last war. He'd want you to have it.

### [MUSIC NO. 06 – WATCH THE MOON]

**YURII.** *(Examines it, hands it back witheringly.)* If it found its way into your hands, I'm sure that's where it should stay.

> *(YURII takes MARKEL aside and speaks quietly.)*

I can't bring all this to the front. Wait until I board the train, then take it home.

> *(Offers money.)*

Look after my family, Markel.

**MARKEL**. *(Hugging* **YURII** *powerfully.)* May God grant you a year more on earth for every life you save, Master!

(**MARKEL** *pulls the cart off.)*

**YURII**. We'd best hurry.

(**TONIA** *stops him.)*

**TONIA**. Yurochka, wait!

(**YURII** *turns back, embraces her.)*

I had a terrible nightmare – you went away and never returned. Be very careful, please.

**YURII**. Everyone agrees the war will be short... and we'll all be home by Christmas.

**TONIA**. Write me long letters so I can picture you as if you were right beside me.

**YURII**. Wherever I am sent, I'll go outside at nightfall and look to the sky... you do the same. That will always be our moment together.

WATCH THE MOON AND THINK OF ME.
LET THE NIGHTS PASS QUICKLY BY.
UNTIL THE DAY THAT I RETURN
YOU'LL WATCH THE MOON AND SO WILL I.

(**YURII** *leaves.* **TONIA** *stays behind.)*

**TONIA**.

WHEN THE WINDS REFUSE TO DIE,
WHEN THE DARK IS EV'RYWHERE,
BEHIND A VEIL OF SILVER CLOUDS,
I'LL WATCH THE MOON AND YOU'LL BE THERE.

(*The scene transitions as* **YURII** *reappears at the war front. He now wears a doctor's lab coat.)*

## Scene 1–5B: Battlefield – By an Infirmary Tent

*(Time has passed.* **YURII** *reads a letter.)*

**YURII & TONIA.**
FROM THE START OF EACH GRAY MORNING
ON THROUGH AFTERNOON,
WHOLE LIFETIMES GO BY
BUT WHEN DUSK DARKENS THE SKY...
I'LL WATCH THE MOON AND THINK OF SPRING,
SIMPLER DAYS WITH TIME TO SPARE.
UNTIL THE DAY YOU'RE IN MY ARMS
I'LL WATCH THE MOON,
AND KNOW YOU'RE THERE.

**YURII.**
I'LL WATCH THE MOON
AND KNOW YOU'RE THERE.

*(***TONIA*** *has faded away. A* **NURSE** *has entered.)*

**NURSE.** We can postpone the operation until morning, doctor.

**YURII.** I'll be fine, thank you.

**NURSE.** But you haven't slept in three days.

**YURII.** Tell me when he's ready.

*(The* **NURSE** *leaves.)*

BY DAYLIGHT I CAN PLAINLY SEE
THE SAVAGERY OF WAR.
BUT ALL THAT NUMBS AND DEADENS ME,
THE MOON HAS SEEN BEFORE.
IT FLOATS ABOVE THE BATTLEFIELD
IMPASSIVE AND IMMUNE
TO ROWS OF MEN THE BATTLE FELLED,

THEIR OPEN EYES COMPELLED...
TO WATCH THE MOON, WITHOUT A CLUE
WHY THEY LIE DEAD AND I SURVIVE.
I PRAY TO GOD I'LL MAKE IT THROUGH,
AND LIVE TO LEARN WHY I'M ALIVE.

*(The* **NURSE** *re-enters.)*

**NURSE.**  Doctor?

*(***YURII** *follows her to surgery.)*

## Scene 1–6: The Battle Front

**Projection Title: 1915 – THE BATTLEFRONT**

**[MUSIC NO. 06A – MARCH TRANSITION]**

(**RUSSIAN SOLDIERS** *enter at a crouch and take up positions in a trench.* **PASHA** *is among the* **SOLDIERS**, *gazing at the enemy through binoculars.*)

**SOLDIERS.** *(Variously.)*
HOLD THIS GROUND FOR THE TSAR!
HOLD THIS GROUND FOR THE TSAR!
HOLD THIS GROUND FOR THE TSAR …!

**LOOKOUT.** No enemy movement out there.

**PASHA.** Maybe the Germans all went home.

*(All the* **SOLDIERS** *laugh.)*

Good idea, why don't we follow their example?

**SOLDIERS.** Ha, ha, ha!

*(A volley of enemy fire silences them.)*

(**PASHA**, *unfazed, scans the battlefield with his binoculars.* **COMMANDER GINTS** *pulls* **PASHA** *down out of the enemy's sightline.*)

(**LIBERIUS**, *a seasoned soldier, turns to a young man beside him,* **YANKO**, *a new recruit.*)

**LIBERIUS.** Steer clear of that Pasha Antipov. He's too damn crazy to be afraid.

(**PASHA** *runs ahead, checks along the trench-line.*)

**GINTS.**  Bad luck, men. There aren't enough rifles to go around. If a man goes down directly ahead, take his. But if he falls to the side, never break ranks. Fight like the Tsar was watching!

**LOOKOUT.**  Ready down the line.

### [MUSIC NO. 07 – FORWARD MARCH FOR THE TSAR]

**GINTS.**
> FORWARD MARCH FOR THE TSAR!
> SHOW THE COWARD KRAUT WHO WE ARE!
> AND WITH GOD ON OUR SIDE
> WE WILL WIN THE FIGHT,
> SEND THE KAISER FLEEING
> TO BERLIN IN FRIGHT!

**GINTS & SOLDIERS.**
> ON THROUGH WIND, RAIN AND COLD!
> NO MORE FEARSOME SIGHT TO BEHOLD
> THAN A STEADFAST HUSSAR
> WITH A SHARP SCIMITAR
> MARCHING FORWARD! FORWARD!
> FORWARD FOR THE TSAR!

**LIBERIUS.**  *(To* **YANKO.***)* Stay close by me, boy. We'll find us a nice deep shell hole and lay low 'til the shooting stops. My name's Liberius.

**YANKO.**  Yanko.

**PASHA.**  And what shell hole do you hide in tomorrow, comrades? 'Til the madness stops there's no place in Russia a bullet won't find you. Take power into your own hands. If we make it through today, come to my meeting tonight...

> *(***SOLDIERS*** pray quietly as* **GINTS** *offers his own private prayer, unheard by the others.)*

**GINTS.**

HEAR MY PRAYER, OH LORD, I BEG OF YOU.
I HAVE NO ONE ELSE TO SAY THIS TO.
WHEN THEY TURN TO ME WITH WEARY EYES
FOR THE WILL TO FIGHT WITH NO SUPPLIES,
HELP ME HIDE MY FEAR OR WE WON'T SURVIVE.
LORD ABOVE, HELP ME KEEP THESE BOYS ALIVE.

(**PASHA** *turns to the disinterested* **LIBERIUS**,
*and the curious* **YOUNG YANKO**.)

**PASHA.**

I DEVOTE MY LIFE TO WIN THE WAR,
BUT IT'S NOT THE TSAR I'M FIGHTING FOR!
IT'S THE BATTLE FOR THE RUSSIAN SOUL,
FOR THE COMMON MAN
TO TAKE CONTROL OF HIS FATE!

(*The prayers of the* **OTHER SOLDIERS**
*overlap.*)

**SOLDIER 1.**

IF I DON'T GET HOME TO TELL MY WIFE,

| **SOLDIER 1.** | **LIBERIUS.** |
|---|---|
| MAY MY LOVED ONES | GUN THAT SHOOTS, |
| KNOW I GAVE MY LIFE | BETTER BOOTS. |

| **SOLDIER 1.** | **SOLDIER 2.** | **PASHA.** |
|---|---|---|
| FOR THE TSAR, | FOR THE TSAR | GUN THAT |
| ALL FOR THE | I PRAY WE | SHOOTS, |
| TSAR, | WIN THE | BETTER BOOTS! |
|  | DAY. |  |

| **GINTS.** | **LIBERIUS & SOLDIERS.** | **OTHER SOLDIERS.** | **PASHA.** |
|---|---|---|---|
| FOR THE | WE'LL BE | LEAD ME | WE'LL BE |
| TSAR | SAFE | SAFE | SAFE |

| I PRAY FOR | THROUGH FLAME | THROUGH FLAME | THROUGH FLAME |
|---|---|---|---|
| **GINTS.** | **LIBERIUS, SOLDIERS & PASHA.** | **SOLDIERS GROUP 2.** | **SOLDIERS GROUP 3.** |
| VICTORY, | AND DANGER. | AND POISON GAS. | AND DANGER. |
| LET ME LEAD | I'M JUST | IF I LIVE TO SEE | NERVES OF IRON |
| MY MEN | FIGHTING FOR | THIS LONG | AND BALLS |
| COURA- GEOUSLY. | MY OWN ASS! | NIGHT PASS. | OF BRASS! |

**YANKO.**

LORD, IF I SHOULD FALL ON THE FIELD OF WAR
WHO WILL KNOW WHERE I AM LYING?
WILL THEY LEAVE ME HERE
TILL THE APRIL THAW?
WILL THERE BE A NAME UPON MY GRAVE?

| **YANKO.** | **OTHERS.** |
|---|---|
| HELP ME HIDE MY FEAR AS THE BULLETS FLY. | AH... |
| SHOW THE OTHER SOLDIERS I AM TRYING. | AH... |
| AND I ONLY PRAY IF I HAVE TO DIE | AH... |
| LET KATARINA KNOW THAT I WAS BRAVE. | FORWARD! FORWARD! FORWARD! FORWARD! |

*(An approaching airplane overhead grows deafening as it passes over and drops mustard gas on the field beyond the trench of the* **SOLDIERS***.)*

**GINTS.** *(Shouts.)* Charge!!

*(With a yell, all climb from the trench and attack.)*

*(The last out is young* **YANKO**.*)*

*(As the* **OTHERS** *charge forward, he pauses in the middle of no-man's-land, stunned by the gunfire, smoke, and noise. A single gunshot fells him. He collapses onto the battlefield.)*

*(The gunfire grows deafening.)*

*(Then, sudden quiet as the scene transitions to...)*

## Scene 1–7: Inside Field Infirmary Tent

### [MUSIC NO. 07A – NURSE ANTIPOVA]

(**YURII** *sits at a desk completing paperwork. There are cots for wounded* **SOLDIERS** *visible behind a curtain. A nurse,* **STEPKA**, *leads a* **WOMAN** *in. It is* **LARA**.)

**STEPKA.** Doctor's busy. Report here in the morning.

(*Pointing.*)

There's an empty cot in back; use that tonight.

(*Starts out.*)

Ask for three trained doctors and what do they send: one volunteer nurse. Typical.

(**STEPKA** *exits.* **LARA** *remains.*)

**LARA.** Larissa Antipova reporting for duty.

**YURII.** (*Too busy to register.*) One moment, please.

(*Then it dawns on each of them who the other is. There is an undeniable electricity to* **LARA**, *he is the strange man from the rain-filled street.*)

| **YURII.** | **LARA.** |
|---|---|
| You're the new volunteer?! Oh my heavens. What on earth are *you* doing here? | I've been helping out along the front line. They said you needed a nurse here. |

**YURII.** (*Uneasy.*) You're a nurse?

**LARA.** Sisters of Mercy. I volunteered.

**YURII**. *(Rallying a little.)* Zhivago. Yurii Andreyech.

**LARA**. *(Recognizing the name, startled.)* Zhivago?!

**YURII**. Did you find your husband?

**LARA**. *(Unprepared; finally.)* No.

**YURII**. I'm so sorry.

**LARA**. *(Opening up despite herself.)* His letters stopped while he was serving in this unit. I'm following every lead I can.

*(Her honesty makes **YURII** speak frankly.)*

**YURII**. About that night...!

**LARA**. Let's forget it happened.

**YURII**. No, please, it's important. Viktor Komarovsky destroyed my father; preyed on all of his weaknesses... gambling, drink, women. He was doing the same to you, wasn't he? And you refused to give him power over you. That night I saw you in the rain – I wanted thank you...

**LARA**. Thank me? For what?

**YURII**. You stood up to him. The way my father never could. If he'd been as strong, he might have saved himself. I've always wanted to be like that, the way you were that night, so sure of what you had to do, so overwhelmed with a passion that the rest of life feels – unimportant.

**LARA**. *(Suddenly vulnerable and awkward.)* I'm sorry to disappoint you but I'm not in the habit of shooting people.

*(Beat.)*

I've interrupted you.

**YURII**. It's nothing. Medical reports, very boring.

**LARA**.  *(With a playful edge.)* Medical reports? Is it possible one of these medical reports appeared in a Moscow poetry pamphlet. Or could there be another Y.A. Zhivago who writes verse?

## [MUSIC NO. 07B – FIELD INFIRMARY]

**YURII**.  *(With wonder.)* You read my poem?

**LARA**.  *(With disbelief.)* 'Searching Through the Rain?' *Everyone's* read it.

**YURII**.  Don't tell the nurses, please. They can't know I write poetry. They'd find it frivolous.

**LARA**.  Are you aware your poem is the talk of Moscow? People copy it by hand and pass it round to friends.

**YURII**.  In times like these poetry's an indulgence; Russia needs doctors, engineers, serious men.

**LARA**.  Poetry isn't serious?

**YURII**.  It's not – *useful.*

> *(Beat.)*

What are they saying? About my poem? In Moscow.

**LARA**.  *(Smiles at his interest.)* Some think the woman in the rain is Russia waiting for better days. But I disagree. I think she's someone you knew. You see into her heart, she's too alive, too real to be an invention.

**YURII**.  She's real. My words didn't do her justice.

> *(In that moment, **LARA**'s guess is confirmed: it is her he's talking about. She is the subject of the poem. She is moved.)*

**LARA**.  I'll report in the morning.

> *(As **LARA** turns to leave, **YANKO**, the boy in uniform shot on the battlefield and wounded,*

*wanders in, clutching a blanket at his abdomen.)*

**YANKO**. *(Puzzled.)* I think I'm hurt.

*(The blanket falls away revealing a bloody abdomen.* **LARA** *and* **YURII** *lay* **YANKO** *on a table.)*

**LARA**. Hold this tight against your stomach, Soldier.

**YANKO**. I don't think it's serious. Can't feel a thing.

**YURII**. He's in shock. If the bleeding doesn't stop, we'll lose him.

**LARA**. Tell me your name, Soldier.

**YANKO**. I'm called Yanko.

**LARA**. Where's your home, Yanko?

**YANKO**. On the map it's called Varchovoy, but we say 'Three Churches' 'cause that's how many was there in the old times.

**YURII**. We'll have to sterilize the wound to see if there's any obstruction.

*(**YURII** gives **LARA** a look: 'It's hopeless, but...')*

Keep him talking.

**LARA**. *(Distracting **YANKO**.)* Do you have a sweetheart back home?

**YANKO**. Katarina. But she doesn't know how I feel. Whenever I try and tell her the words stick in my throat.

**LARA**. When you're up and about, write and tell her everything. She'll be happy, I promise you.

**YURII**. Ready. Hold him firmly.

*(**YURII** reaches in and gently... tugs!)*

**YANKO.** *(A heartrending scream.)*

> *(***YANKO*** *sits suddenly rigid, then sinks unconscious on the gurney.* **YURII** *holds a piece of metal in his forceps.* **LARA** *checks his vital signs. A pause. Against all odds,* **YANKO** *will survive.)*

**YURII.** It passed clean through him.

**LARA.** His pulse is steady.

**YURII.** *(Looks at her.)* A miracle.

## Scene 1–8: Study in the Gromeko House

**[MUSIC NO. 08 – HOME WHERE THE LILACS GROW]**

(**TONIA** *reads a letter aloud to* **ALEX** *and* **ANNA** *while* **MARKEL** *takes* **TONIA** *and* **YURII**'s *baby from* **ANNA** *and rocks it gently.*)

**TONIA**. *(Reads the letter aloud.)* 'Dearest Tonyechka, the war grinds on with unimaginable carnage. I fear at times that I'll never live to meet our son, and it saddens me beyond words. I'm still having heart palpitations, but my condition responds well to a new medication. At the front, these small mercies are all we dare hope for. A new volunteer nurse arrived, Antipova's her name. Her quiet goodness and industry have a soothing effect on everyone's mood...'

(**TONIA** *passes the letter to* **ANNA** *and* **ALEX**. *Music continues as the scene transitions to...*)

## Scene 1-8B: Nurse's Quarters, The Front

> (**NURSES** *iron linens with* **LARA**. **OLYA**, *a homesick nurse, plays the concertina and hums.*)

**OLYA.**
MMM-HMM-HMM-HMM-HMM.
MMM-HMM-HMM.
MMM-HMM-HMM-HMM-HMM.
MMM-HMM-HMM.

> (*She continues playing the concertina quietly.* **STEPKA**, *the garrulous nurse, on a break, eats.*)

**STEPKA.**  Some of us nurses are shipping south to a new unit, that's the talk.

**VARYA.**  Did the doctor say anything to you, Larissa Antipova?

**LARA.**  (*Slightly prim.*) He tells me nothing he wouldn't tell you.

**STEPKA.**  But with her he makes it rhyme.

> (*Other* **NURSES** *chuckle.*)

**LARA.**  (*Used to this teasing.*) Finish eating, Stepka. Varya's due for a break.

**VARYA.**  I can think of one nurse who won't be sent south... unless the doctor goes.

**LARA.**  (*Amused/embarrassed.*) If we'd spend more time working, and less time in idle gossip, we might get to bed in time for a decent night's sleep, for once.

**MARFA.**  Why do you think she wants to be in bed sooner?

**STEPKA.**  My bed has fleas in it.

**VARYA.** Hers must have something else.

*(**YURII** bursts in holding a news sheet which he has just finished reading.)*

**YURII.** Have you seen the news sheet? 'Draftees at the Petrograd barracks refuse orders to ship to the front, join students radicals and workers in protest of the Tsar's suicidal war.'

*(**LARA** and the **NURSES** gather round.)*

**MARFA.** If no soldiers show up, who's going to fight the war?

**YURII.** Exactly. Without men the war is over.

**LARA.** The Tsar will have no choice. Negotiate a peace, or surrender to Germany.

**STEPKA.** I'm confused. What does it mean?

**YURII.** It means... we're going home!

*(A pause. **VARYA** bursts into tears. Stunned, the **NURSES** study the news sheet.)*

**VARYA.** Is it possible?

**LARA.** Imagine, Stepka, you'll smell the ocean again.

**STEPKA.** My Odessa...

**MARFA.** My Kyiv...

**OLYA.** My husband...

*(**OLYA** begins to sing a capella.)*

ARE YOU STILL REMEMBERING ME?
I PRAY IT'S SO,
DANCING ALL NIGHT IN THE MOONLIGHT,
HOME WHERE THE LILACS GROW.

*(Other **NURSES** join in, all except **LARA**.)*

**OLYA & NURSES.**

WARRING WINDS HAVE TORN US APART
LONG YEARS AGO.
NOW ONLY A DREAM CAN TAKE ME
HOME WHERE THE LILACS GROW.

(The **NURSES** harmonize under **OLYA**.)

| **OLYA.** | **NURSES.** |
|---|---|
| FIELDS OF SWEETNESS | AH |
|    FILL THE AIR, | |
| BURSTING OPEN TO | AH. |
|    BLOOM AS THEY DARE. | |

**OLYA & NURSES.**

HERE WHERE THE SNOW COVERS EV'RYTHING,
I YEARN FOR SPRING AND HOPE RETURNING...
LIKE A SEED ASLEEP IN THE GROUND,
LOVE LONGS TO SHOW.
TELL ME YOU'LL STILL BE WAITING
HOME WHERE THE LILACS GROW.
TELL ME YOU'LL STILL BE WAITING
HOME WHERE THE LILACS GROW.

(**MARFA** sweeps **YURII** into a dance. The **OTHER NURSES** take nightshirts up as if they were men and start dancing with them. They are each passed from nurse to nurse as the music speeds into a celebratory whirl.)

(**YURII** and **LARA** get caught in each other's gaze, and then they begin to dance, at first stiffly, and then, as the music swells, they whirl around faster and faster, dancing with abandon.)

OH, THESE DAYS, THESE NIGHTS, THESE DAYS,
SPINNING AROUND TILL MY MIND IS A MAZE.
YEARNING TO HOLD YOU AND LEAD YOU TO
THE HOME WE KNEW AND LOVED SO DEARLY...

*(At last **YURII** and **LARA** realize that everyone else has stopped dancing and is watching them, bemused. **YURII** exits, embarrassed.)*

**LARA.**
CAN YOU HEAR THE SONG THAT I SING,
URGENT AND LOW?

**OLYA & NURSES.**
TELL ME YOU'LL STILL BE WAITING
HOME WHERE THE LILACS GROW.
WE'LL DANCE THROUGH THE NIGHT
IN THE MOONLIGHT,
HOME WHERE THE LILACS GROW.

*(Returning to the ironing board, **LARA** realizes with a smile that in her distraction, she has allowed the iron to burn a mark onto a shirt. She shows it to the other **NURSES**.)*

*(Then there is a loud battlefield explosion. The **NURSES** scatter.)*

*(The scene transitions to...)*

## Scene 1–9: Rail Siding Near the Front Line

### [MUSIC NO. 09 – FORWARD MARCH (REPRISE)]

### Projection Title: OCTOBER 1917

*(Amidst the sounds of chaos and explosions,* **SOLDIERS** *run helter-skelter, a confused retreat, shouting over the music.* **COMMANDER GINTS** *tries to push them off a railway car when they try to clamber aboard.)*

**SOLDIER ONE**.  Germans broke through the north perimeter! We're done for!

**SOLDIER TWO**.  We can't retreat without orders!

**SOLDIER ONE**.  To hell with orders! There's the supply train, take it over, and let's move out!

**SOLDIERS**. *(Variously.)*  Evacuate the lines!! Retreat!! Retreat!! Retreat!!

> *(A* **QUARTERMASTER** *tries to block them.)*

**GINTS**.  No, the line's holding; it's a small breach. We can regroup and counter-attack!

> *(The* **SOLDIERS** *reluctantly re-form ranks, returning to battle as* **YURII** *and* **LARA** *enter with* **NURSES** *carrying medical supplies for evacuation.)*

> *(The train station* **QUARTERMASTER** *supervises loading a train.* **YURII** *and* **LARA** *approach.* **YURII** *presents orders to the* **QUARTERMASTER**.*)*

**YURII.** We've been assigned a rail car to evacuate the wounded.

> (*The* **QUARTERMASTER** *'examines' the orders, then hands them back.*)

**QUARTERMASTER.** News to me.

**LARA.** These men will die if we leave them behind.

**YURII.** You can't refuse a written order.

> (**QUARTERMASTER** *shrugs. Then, to* **LARA** ...)

We'll have to check further back.

> (*As* **YURII** *starts to leave,* **LARA** *approaches the* **QUARTERMASTER** *with money.*)

**LARA.** Listen, brother. Be on the lookout for these counterfeit rubles; some men are trying to pass them off for a place on the sick list.

**QUARTERMASTER.** (*Inspecting the notes.*) There's nothing wrong with this money!

**LARA.** If you're caught spending it, don't point a finger at me.

> (**QUARTERMASTER** *grins, takes the money.*)

Now where'd you say we could put the wounded?

**QUARTERMASTER.** (*Points off down the train.*) Empty flatbed – third back from the engine.

**YURII.** (*To the* **NURSE**.) Load the most severe cases first.

**NURSE.** Yes, Doctor.

> (*The evacuation is finally under way.* **YURII** *and* **LARA** *know it's time to part.*)

**YURII.** Thank you, Nurse Antipova. I don't know what we'd have done without you.

*(Lost for words.)*

If our paths ever cross in Moscow –

**LARA**. I'm not going back there.

**YURII**. Why not?

**LARA**. Too many memories. I'm returning to where I was born – the Ural Mountains. Pasha and I had plans to teach there together one day. Yuriatin.

**YURII**. Yuriatin?

**LARA**. *(Wistfully.)* It's... tiny. Peaceful. I'll find work, live quietly.

**YURII**. I'm very sorry the war took your husband.

> *(Now that they'll never see each other again,*
> *she can finally speak her heart.)*

**LARA**. We were never truly *married*.

**YURII**. *(Guessing.)* But you risked your life trying to find him.

**LARA**. I was trying to be worthy of his love.

**YURII**. Worthy?

**LARA**. *(Almost to herself.)* I've done so many unforgivable things, doctor.

## [MUSIC NO. 09A – YANKO'S DEATH]

Things I'd like to forget.

**YURII**. You need no forgiveness, Lara.

**LARA**. You don't know me.

**YURII**. I know that all you've done til now is part of who you've become, and what I see is radiant and good.

**LARA.** *(Trying to pull away from the intensity.)* No more, Yurii Andreyevich. It's enough that we met. I'll read your poetry. I'll be proud I knew you...

**YURII.** Lara...

**LARA.** Say good-bye before we do something we'll both regret.

> *(They stand immobilized by their feelings. Explosions. **SOLDIERS** flee across the stage.)*

**SOLDIER.** The Huns broke through!

> *(**YANKO** enters with an eerily peaceful smile, in no pain at all.)*

**YURII.** Yanko...?

**YANKO.** *(Detached.)* You patch me all up nice, and the Germans go and mess up your good work.

> *(**YANKO** sinks to his knees and topples over. **YURII** lifts him onto the train. **YANKO** dies. **YURII** closes **YANKO**'s eyes.)*

**YURII.** He turned fifteen last week. Lied to get in the army, he told me.

**LARA.** Poor child.

> *(**LARA** finds a letter tucked under his tunic. She reads the envelope.)*

"If you find this letter, please send it to Katarina in the village of Varchovoy."

> *(She shows **YURII** the letter. He reads it.)*

**[MUSIC NO. 10 – NOW]**

**YURII.** Dear Katarina...

I'M LYING IN THIS TENT
AND THERE' S NOT MUCH LIGHT
AND I CANNOT WRITE FOR LONG
BUT THESE WORDS I'VE NEVER SAID
KEEP HAUNTING ME
AND I KNOW THEY CAN'T BE WRONG.
AND I'M STILL A LITTLE SHY
TO SPEAK MY MIND
BUT THE TRUTH JUST WON'T STAY DOWN.
FOR HERE IN THE NIGHT
THERE'S NO WRONG AND NO RIGHT.
THERE IS ONLY THE DARK.
I'M ALONE WITH MY HEART...

AND NOW, I NEED TO TELL YOU NOW
I NEED TO TELL YOU HOW
YOU MAKE ME FEEL.
YOU'RE LIKE A SONG.
I SING YOU ALL DAY LONG.
A MELODY SO STRONG
AND SWEET AND REAL.
AND I DON'T KNOW
IF YOU'LL EVER FEEL THIS WAY
BUT I HAVE TO SAY
WHAT I HAVE TO SAY
I LOVE YOU.
AND I NEED TO TELL YOU NOW.

**LARA.** *(Takes letter, reads it.)*

I WONDER IF YOU KNEW
EV'RY TIME WE MET
I WAS TREMBLING INSIDE.
I LONGED TO TAKE YOUR HAND
FOR WE STOOD SO CLOSE
BUT THE DISTANCE SEEMED SO WIDE.
I WAS WAITING FOR A TIME,

A TURN, A SIGN,
AS THE DAYS KEPT RUSHING BY.
AND IT ALL WENT SO FAST,
THE MOMENT HAD PASSED
AND I KNOW THAT YOU'RE GONE
BUT THE HUNGER LIVES ON ...
AND NOW, I NEED TO TELL YOU NOW.
I NEED TO TELL YOU HOW
YOU MAKE ME FEEL.
THERE'S ONLY NOW.
WHAT POINT IS THERE TO WAIT?
TOMORROW IS TOO LATE.
I CAN'T CONCEAL
THAT I MAY NOT EVER HAVE ANOTHER DAY
SO I HAVE TO SAY WHAT I HAVE TO SAY.
I LOVE YOU, AND I NEED TO TELL YOU NOW.

**YURII.**
MY ARMS ARE EMPTY

**LARA.**
BUT YOU'RE STILL HERE

**BOTH.**
LIKE A MIRAGE THAT WILL DISAPPEAR.

*(They break free of the letter, and sing to each other.)*

**YURII & LARA.**
NOW, THE ONLY TIME IS NOW.
A TIME TO TELL YOU HOW
I NEED YOU NEAR.
I BREATHE YOU IN.
I FEEL YOU ON MY SKIN.
YOU MELT AWAY THE COLD
AND PAIN AND FEAR.
AND THERE MAY NOT EVER BE ANOTHER DAY
BUT I KNOW MY LIFE CAN'T END THIS WAY
I LOVE YOU ...

**YURII.**
AND I NEED TO TELL YOU NOW...

**LARA.**
I NEED TO TELL YOU...

**YURII & LARA.**
I NEED TO TELL YOU NOW.

> *(They embrace and kiss. With a supreme effort,* **LARA** *turns away to leave. Explosions rend the air.*

### [MUSIC NO. 11 – BLOOD ON THE SNOW]

> *(***SOLDIERS** *flood on from the direction of 'battle.'* **LIBERIUS** *leads.)*

**SOLDIER ONE.** They Germans, they're overrunning the camp! Clear out!

> *(***LARA**'s gone. **YURII**, *still dazed by her abrupt disappearance, slowly notes the chaotic retreat. A* **WOUNDED SOLDIER** *passes by, confused.)*

**YURII.** Come with me.

> *(***YURII** *leads the* **WOUNDED SOLDIER** *off.)*

**LIBERIUS.** Keep what you can carry, leave the rest behind!

> *(***GINTS** *jumps onto the train to stop* **SOLDIERS** *from fleeing.)*

**GINTS.** No, men! Back to the front. Replacements are coming!

| **GINTS.** | **SOLDIERS.** |
| --- | --- |
| ON THROUGH WIND, | Rot in hell! |

RAIN AND COLD!
NO MORE FEARSOME
   SIGHT TO BEHOLD
THAN A STEADFAST
   HUSSAR,
WITH A SHARP SCIMITAR
MARCHING FORWARD!
FORWARD!!
FORWARD ...!

Hang you, hang the
army!
Hang the war!
Where was God when
we needed him?
When our Brothers were
turned into canon
fodder?
Retreat! Retreat!
Retreat! Retreat!

**GINTS.** I order you forward!

> (*A gunshot.* **GINTS** *falls like a rag onto the train. Stunned silence as* **SOLDIERS** *turn to see who fired. It is none other than* **PASHA**. *Forcefully, taking charge, he lowers his rifle.*)

**PASHA.**
BLOOD ON THE SNOW,
THE BLOOD OF OUR BROTHERS
SPILLED FOR A WAR
THERE IS NO PURPOSE FOR.
I WILL LAY DOWN MY GUN
THOUGH SOME CALL IT TREASON –

**PASHA & LIBERIUS.**
WHY SHOULD I DIE
WHEN I DON'T HAVE A REASON?

**PASHA, LIBERIUS & ONE SOLDIER.**
ONE MORE DEATH MEANS NOTHING TO ANYONE.

**PASHA & SOLDIERS.**
HOMEWARD I GO, A SOLDIER NO LONGER,
WEARY BUT STRONGER
MY DAYS ON THE BATTLEFIELD ARE DONE.

>*(**PASHA** steps forward and sees **YANKO** laying dead on the train, his chest bloody. With sadness and fury, **PASHA** soaks his handkerchief in **YANKO**'s blood, fashions it into a red band knotted around his arm.)*

**PASHA.**
*NOW* IT BEGINS!
TRUE REVOLUTION,
RAGING FOR ALL THE WORLD TO SEE!
THIS BLOODIED RAG,
OUR FLAG OF HONOR,
SYMBOL OF SOLIDARITY!
YOU AND I, THE PEOPLE'S ARMY!
YOU AND I, THE PEOPLE'S ARMY!
HOMEWARD I GO, A SOLDIER NO LONGER,
WEARY BUT STRONGER
MY DAYS ON THE BATTLEFIELD ARE DONE!

>*(**LIBERIUS** follows suit as more blood-soaked armbands are made as **SOLDIERS** knot them onto their arms.)*

FLAME OF FREEDOM

**PASHA & SOLDIERS.**
BLAZE ACROSS THE PLAIN
TO THE HORIZON.

>*(**SOLDIERS** and **NURSES** help each other onto the train as it pulls away.)*

| **SOLDIERS & NURSES.** | **PASHA, LIBERIUS & SOLDIERS.** |
|---|---|
| BLOOD ON THE SNOW, | *NOW* IT BEGINS! |
| THE BLOOD OF OUR BROTHERS | TRUE REVOLUTION, |

SPILLED FOR A WAR
THERE IS NO PURPOSE
 FOR.
COMRADES, LAY DOWN
 YOUR GUNS
TO FIGHT IN A NEW WAY
RED SUN AGLOW IT'S THE
 DAWN OF A NEW DAY!
PEACE AND BREAD
AND FREE LAND FOR
 EV'RYONE!
PEACE AND BREAD
AND FREE LAND FOR
 EV'RYONE!
HOMEWARD I GO,
A SOLDIER NO LONGER.
WISER AND STRONGER,
THE FIGHT FOR THE
 FUTURE HAS BEGUN!

RAGING FOR ALL THE
 WORLD TO SEE!

THIS BLOODIED RAG,

OUR FLAG OF HONOR,
SYMBOL OF SOLIDARITY!

HANG THE TSAR
AND SPARE THE ARMY!

HANG THE TSAR
AND SPARE THE ARMY!

HOMEWARD WE GO,
ARMY NO LONGER.
WISER

THE FUTURE'S BEGUN!

(**NURSES** & **SOLDIERS** *and the bodies of* **GINTS** *and* **YANKO** *ride off on the departing train.*)

(*During the transition, the orchestral music of* **[BLOOD ON THE SNOW]** *changes character, as it does throughout the ensuing scene, echoing the corruption of the early revolutionary ideals.*)

(*As the train moves off,* **YURII** *runs back and is stranded alone on stage with only his duffel bag. He picks it up and turns.*)

(**YURII** *is now back in...*)

## Scene 1–10: Gromeko House – Grand Hall

### Projection Title: JANUARY 1918

*(Last seen grandly furnished at the beginning
of the play, the Grand Hall is now derelict,
stripped clean by marauders. Chairs are
piled in a heap.)*

**YURII.** *(Calling.)* Hello? Tonia? Markel? Nana?

*(A tiny sinister man appears;* **SHULYGIN.***)*

Who are you?

**SHULYGIN.** No, comrade, the question is; who are you?
May we see identification?

*(***GOLYUBOVA***, large and placid, enters.)*

**YURII.** This is my home.

*(***TONIA*** *enters from outdoors with* **ANNA***,
***ALEX*** *and* **SASHA***, all heavily bundled in
threadbare coats.* **MARKEL** *enters from
upstairs.)*

**GOLYUBOVA.** *(To* **TONIA***.)* Comrade Zhivago, you have an
unauthorized visitor.

**YURII.** *(When* **TONIA** *doesn't register him...)* Tonia?

**TONIA.** Oh dear God in Heaven, is it really you?

**MARKEL.** *(Deeply moved, hobbling towards him.)* Young
master...

*(***YURII*** *and* **TONIA** *embrace.)*

**YURII.** Why are these strangers in our house? Where are
the servants?

**MARKEL**. *(Whispering, he thinks inaudibly.)* Sir, the Tsar's in prison, and most of the better families fled Moscow...

**TONIA**. Quiet, Markel.

> *(A warning look to him, then an apologetic appeal for their old retainer's outburst, and she changes the subject:)*

Sasha, come say hello to your father!

**SASHA**. *(A shy approach, then he stops.)* I don't know you.

> *(***ALEX*** follows **MARKEL**.)*

**ANNA**. *(Following **ALEX**.)* Welcome home, Son!

## [MUSIC NO. 12 – THE PERFECT WORLD]

**TONIA**. This is Comrade Shulygin and Comrade Golyubova who have honored us by choosing our home as headquarters of the Worker's Agricultural Research Institute. They keep an eye on everything day and night.

**YURII**. They took our home?!

**TONIA**. We're allowed the use of the entire top floor.

**YURII**. What, the attic!

**SHULYGIN**.
YOURS IS NOT TO SAY WHAT IS YOURS, WHAT IS NOT.

**GOLYUBOVA**.
WHAT IS WHAT IS THE SAY OF THE PEOPLE.

**YURII**. What's going on here, Tonia?

**GOLYUBOVA**.
WE HAVE BEEN ASSIGNED TO DECIDE...

**SHULYGIN**.
TO DIVIDE...

**GOLYUBOVA.**
WHAT YOU NEED TO SUBSIST...

**SHULYGIN.**
JUST ENOUGH TO EXIST.

**BOTH.**
EV'RYONE WILL HAVE EV'RYTHING THEY NEED.

**SHULYGIN.**
EV'RYONE THE SAME.
ANY MORE WOULD BE GREED!

| **GOLYUBOVA.** | **SHULYGIN.** |
|---|---|
| EV'RYONE HAS GOT | |
| A PORTION OF THE POT. | FEED THE NEEDY! |
| IF JUST A LITTLE | THE NEEDY! |
| IS THE MOST WE'VE GOT, | |
| | NOT TO BE SELFISH. |

**BOTH.**
GETTING JUST A LITTLE IS A LOT!

**YURII.**  But the attic –

**TONIA.**  – is more than adequate. We've kept your desk in the corner, so you can write.

*(Covering, to* **SHULYGIN** *&* **GOLYUBOVA.***)*

My husband is a celebrated poet, you know.

**GOLYUBOVA.**  *(With unctuous authority.)* We know all about your husband's poetry, Comrade Zhivago.

**GOLYUBOVA, SHULYGIN & OTHERS IN THE HOUSE.**
IN THE PERFECT WORLD,
THE SYSTEM HAS TO RUN
FOR THE GOOD OF ALL, NOT SOME.
IN THE PERFECT WORLD,
WE ALL MUST THINK AS ONE

**GOLYUBOVA & SHULYGIN.**

    IF PERFECTION IS TO COME
    IN THE PERFECT WORLD.

## Scene 1–10B: Cultural Affairs Committee

(**PARTY OFFICIALS** *enter for a committee hearing on* **YURII***'s poetry.* **YURII** *stands before them as he is questioned. On nearby chairs, several other* **WRITERS** *sit awaiting interrogation.*)

**OFFICIAL ONE**. We are asking a simple question. Comrade; what exactly does your poetry *MEAN*?!

**YURII**. It depends on the poem, it means different things to different people.

**OFFICIAL TWO**. Such clever answers no doubt impress your aristocratic literary friends, Comrade Zhivago. But the Writer's Committee needs more *clarity* on your position.

**YURII**. I think my 'position' in a poem is a personal matter –

**OFFICIAL ONE**.
YOURS IS NOT TO 'THINK'
TO "REVIEW" OR 'OPINE'
BUT TO HEW TO THE LINE OF THE PARTY!

**YURII**. If I might, my friend –

**OFFICIAL TWO**.
PATRONIZING WORDS CAN OFFEND.

**OFFICIAL THREE**.
SUCH AS 'FRIEND.'

**OFFICIAL ONE**.
'FRIEND' IS BAD.

**OFFICIAL TWO**.
SAY 'COMRADE.'

**OFFICIAL THREE**.
AND OF COURSE,

**ALL THREE.**
'LENINGRAD!'

**COMMITTEE.** *(Variously.)*

| | |
|---|---|
| EV'RYONE BELONGS TO A SINGLE CLASS. BOURGEOIS DAYS ARE DONE! | WE ARE ONE SINGLE CLASS! |
| NO ONE MAY CREATE WORDS THAT CAUSE DEBATE! | YOU'RE A LIGHTWEIGHT! |

**OFFICIAL ONE.**        **COMMITTEE.**

| | |
|---|---|
| LANGUAGE MUST UNIFY THE CLASS-LESS STATE! | OR ORATE! |

**COMMITTEE.**
SENTIMENTAL VERSE IS OUT-OF-DATE!

**YURII.** What I write is no business of yours, no disrespect intended.

**OFFICIAL THREE.** What would the son of an imperialist factory owner know about respect! The Zhivago family has exploited the workers for generations –

**YURII.** *(Controlled.)* I am not my father.

> (**KOMAROVSKY** *rises from among the officials. He looks decidedly more proletarian now than he did before the revolution.*)

**KOMAROVSKY.** Comrade, if I may...

**OFFICIAL ONE.** Citizen Advocate Komarovsky, please...

**KOMAROVSKY.** We all know that even the most private poems invite political interpretation.

**YURII.** I'm not a political poet.

**KOMAROVSKY.** May I finish...

**YURII.** I can't control what readers think –

**KOMAROVSKY.** *(To* **YURII.***)* While you were fighting for the *Tsar*, you were spared the people's struggle for Russia's future here in Moscow. You've enjoyed the fruits of our struggle, but not made the sacrifices. Perhaps in the future your work will more clearly *celebrate* the People's Revolution...

> *(To the others.)*

Might this not influence our decision, Comrades?

> *(To* **YURII.***)*

ODES TO ROMANTIC LOVE ARE BANNED.
IT'S LOVE OF *NATION* WE DEMAND.
KEEP THE FLAMES OF REVOLUTION FANNED
AS WE BUILD THE PERFECT WORLD.

**COMMITTEE.** *(Ad lib.)* Hear, hear!

**OFFICIAL ONE.**
ONE MANIFESTO, AND NO DISSENT!

**OFFICIAL TWO.**
WE'VE DECREED
RUSSIANS NEED
ART THAT BREEDS CONTENT!

**COMMITTEE.** *(Variously.)*
THE WORKER AT HIS FORGE!
THE PEASANT AT HIS PLOUGH!
THE HAMMER AND THE SICKLE, UNITED NOW
AS A BRIGHT NEW DAY
OF FREEDOM IS UNFURLED
IN THE FLAG OF THE PARTY!

> *(***KOMAROVSKY*** speaks with special emphasis.)*

**KOMAROVSKY.** All across Russia, so many abandoned chairs where writers once sat. How we'd hate to see yours unoccupied only because you couldn't follow the correct path.

**YURII.** *(Gets the point.)* Henceforth, my verse will follow the 'correct path' Comrade Komarovsky.

> *(The **FOUR WRITERS** in chairs, fallen out of favor, are marched forward and blindfolded. In horror **YURII** recognizes one of them, **NIKOLAI**, his publisher, now hollow-eyed and gaunt. **YURII** utters a strangled cry.)*

Nikolai, no!!

**NIKOLAI.** Yurii!! Ahhhhh!

**ALL.**
IN THE PERFECT WORLD
ALL WORKERS WILL ARISE
IN A DREAM OF MARX FULFILLED!
REVOLUTION WON, WE LIFT A NATION'S EYES
TO THE FUTURE WE WILL BUILD
IN THE PERFECT WORLD!
IN THE PERFECT WORLD!
THE PERFECT WORLD!

> *(**YURII** watches in horror as **FOUR WRITERS** are led out and executed as we hear the echoes of the firing squad.)*

## Scene 1–11: A Street in Moscow

### [MUSIC NO. 12A – KOMAROVSKY'S LAMENT]

*(Stunned,* **YURII** *steps outside, his face ashen. He is deep in thought.* **KOMAROVSKY** *weaves beside* **YURII***, flask in hand, drunk.)*

**KOMAROVSKY**.  Learn to bend, Zhivago. I can't protect you forever.

**YURII**.  How can you live like this?

**KOMAROVSKY**.  *(A drunken ramble.)* I'm a guardian angel, sent from above to keep my friends safe. You think your principles make you virtuous? *This* is virtue, in *here*.

> *(Pounds his breastbone.)*

And does anyone notice, much less *thank* me? I've been slandered, vilified, even shot at once, and by a dressmaker's daughter! Imagine. A common seamstress.

**YURII**.  I was there!

**KOMAROVSKY**.  *(Suddenly brightens.)* That's right.

> *(Stops, and* **YURII** *turns away from him distressed by the memory.)*

Poor creature. Lost her husband in the war, you know.

> *(***YURII*** *looks back at* **KOMAROVSKY** *with sudden focus.* **KOMAROVSKY** *notices, and changes the subject. He reaches into his pocket and pulls out...)*

Look! An egg. Take it. Feed your son.

**YURII**.  You're drunk.

**KOMAROVSKY.** How else could anyone tolerate life in the nightmare country Russia has become...

HOW COULD THIS HAVE HAPPENED?
MOSCOW UP IN SMOKE.
EV'RYTHING WE CHERISHED,
SHATTERED, NOW A SORDID JOKE.
THE LAUGHTER. THE MUSIC.
THE CAVIAR, THE CREAM...
AND THE GIRLS IN WHITE BY CANDLELIGHT.
ALL A DISTANT DREAM.

*(He turns to* **YURII** *for confirmation, but he is alone.* **YURII** *has gone to...)*

## Scene 1-12: Gromeko's Attic

*(One small room.* **ALEX**, **ANNA**, **SASHA**, **YURII** *and* **TONIA** *are seated for dinner.* **TONIA** *passes a serving plate with miniscule portions which each of them take.* **YURII** *is remote, lost in thought.)*

**ALEX**.  Tonight we once again re-enact The Great Mystery of the Worker's Revolution. We each have a fork.

*(Holds up the fork.)*

We each have a plate.

*(Holds up the plate.)*

But where's the *food*?

**TONIA**.  Yurii? Take your soup. It's good for your heart.

*(***YURII*** *hasn't taken a bite for himself.)*

**YURII**.  Give my portion to Sasha.

**TONIA**.  My poor darling. You're so far away. Tell me what's troubling you?

**ANNA**.  Why's it so cold?

*(As* **ALEX** *pulls her shawl tight around her,* **YURII** *rises:)*

**YURII**.  I'll find wood for the fire.

**TONIA**.  Eat first. You need your strength.

**YURII**.  *(Quiet bitterness.)* Look at us. All I ever wanted was to keep my family safe... and I can't even keep us from starvation.

**ANNA**.  *(In a reverie.)* We used to serve seven courses at dinner.

**ALEX**. *(Watching* **ANNA***.)* The old summer home, the Kruger Estate... she keeps wandering back there in her mind –

**ANNA**. *(Interrupting.)* How I loved the mountains. Everything belonged to us, rivers, forests...

**YURII**. What do you think became of that place?

**ALEX**. Rotting into the ground, no doubt, like all Russia since the glorious workers took over –

**ANNA**. *(Interjects.)* It's where it always was; some things never change, thank Heaven.

**YURII**. *(Seized by an idea.)* If it's abandoned, why couldn't *we* move there? Grow our own food. There'd be no one spying on us. I might even write again.

**TONIA**. Yes!

**ALEX**. We were good to our people there. I'm sure they'd welcome us.

**YURII**. I'll arrange the train fare. In the meantime, not a word to anyone. To them, we're all White Russians, loyal to the Tsar. If they find out we're leaving Moscow, they'll arrest us all.

**ANNA**. *(Growing more focused.)* Wire ahead, and tell the overseer to meet us at Yuriatin.

**YURII**. *(Startled by the name.)* Yuriatin?

## [MUSIC NO. 13 – YURII'S DECISION]

**ALEX**. It's the nearest station, only half a day's ride from the Estate.

**YURII**. *(Suddenly alarmed, making excuses.)* Yuriatin... I didn't realize. We can't go there. The Red Army's out of control in that district!

**TONIA.** *(Rising to find a newspaper.)* But the newspapers are saying that the White Army has control of the Eastern Urals now –

**YURII.** *(Now agitated.)* Enough! It's too dangerous. I'll find firewood…

> *(***YURII*** *hurries into the street with his umbrella. Thunder.* ***SASHA*** *remains on stage for* ***YURII***'s *walk; a reminder of the family* ***YURII*** *must protect, an image in* ***YURII***'s *imagination.)*

> *(Through the song,* ***YURII*** *passes* ***MUSCOVITES*** *in the streets, young lovers, the destitute, but mostly, like an obsessive vision, a* ***WOMAN*** *whose form haunts him.)*

## Scene 1–12B: Streets of Moscow

**YURII.**
WHY OF ALL THE PLACES IN THE WORLD?
WHO OF ALL THE PEOPLE TO BE LIVING THERE?
DASHING ALL THE CAREFUL PLANS
OF A CONSCIENTIOUS MAN
WHO TRIED TO LEAVE THINGS AS THEY WERE.
AFTER EV'RY TOUCH WE NEVER FELT,
AFTER EV'RY WORD WE LEFT UNSPOKEN,
WHY IS HEAVEN TESTING ME?
IS IT CHANCE OR DESTINY
THAT THIS ROAD LEADS ONLY TO HER?

*(The* **WOMAN** *stands in the street, her back to him.)*

DAY AFTER DAY, YEAR AFTER YEAR
CAN I RESIST WHEN SHE IS NEAR?

*(She turns. She is not* **LARA**. *He paces the street trying to convince himself of the right thing to do.)*

ALL MY LIFE I HAVE TRIED TO LIVE WITH HONOR
AND BE FREE FROM THE SHADOW OF DISGRACE.

*(Another* **WOMAN** *passes, and another.)*

BUT LIKE FATHER, LIKE SON,
IT'S ALREADY BEGUN.
EV'RYWHERE I TURN,
I STILL SEE HER FACE...
FOR THE SAKE OF MY FAM'LY'S SURVIVAL
I WILL SILENCE THE BEATING OF MY HEART,
FOR A MAN IS DEFINED
BY THE STRENGTH OF HIS MIND,
BY THE SUM OF HIS DEEDS,
WHEN HIS DREAMS FALL APART!

*(The **WOMAN** haunting him pauses as **YURII** looks at her for the last time. The sun rises in the street.)*

LEAVE THE STARS IN THE SKY.
LET THE NIGHT FIRES DIE.
HIDE THE SUN IN A CLOUD OF GRAY...
AND IF EVER I SHOULD MEET HER
ON A VILLAGE STREET,
I'LL VERY CALMLY TURN
AND WALK THE OTHER WAY...

I AM YURII ANDREYEVICH ZHIVAGO!
I WILL NOT LEAVE A LEGACY OF SHAME!
FOR A MAN IS DEFINED
BY THE STRENGTH OF HIS MIND.
BY HIS MORAL FOUNDATION
IN THE FACE OF TEMPTATION,
AND BY GOD, WHEN I DIE
LET MY SON KNOW THAT I
WAS A MAN WHO LIVED UP TO HIS NAME!
A MAN WHO LIVED UP TO HIS NAME!

*(**YURII** is back in the attic, and reaches out to hold **SASHA** close to him, a man determined to honor what is expected of him.)*

We're about to take a long train ride, son. And where we're going, we'll both need to be very, very strong.

### [MUSIC NO. 14 – IN THIS HOUSE]

*(We hear the sound of distant chimes. The family prepares to escape Moscow.)*

## Scene 1–13: Gromeko's Attic

### Projection Title: TWO WEEKS LATER

*(**ALEX** enters holding **ANNA**'s shawl, which he drapes over her chair, and pats fondly.)*

**ALEX.** Good-bye my dear. Perhaps it's better you were spared this journey. What will I do without you to finish my sentences?

> *(**YURII**, **TONIA**, and **SASHA** enter wearing layers of clothing. **YURII** checks out the window.)*

**YURII.** The street's clear.

**TONIA.** Sasha, it's time to say good-bye to our home.

**SASHA.** I don't want to leave!

**TONIA.** We may not see this place again for a very long time, darling.

**YURII.** *(Understanding.)* Let him say goodbye his own way.

**SASHA.**
HOUSE, DON'T BE FRIGHTENED
WHEN I'M FAR AWAY.
TELL THE BOY WHO TAKES MY BED
I'LL BE BACK SOME DAY.
HOUSE, I MUST LEAVE YOU
EV'RYTHING I OWN
ALL EXCEPT MY MEM'RIES
THOSE ARE MINE ALONE.

> *(**ALEX** looks around, a farewell to his home.)*

**ALEX.**
IN THIS HOUSE, I STILL HEAR HER FOOTSTEPS.
VELVET SHOES DANCING DOWN THE STAIR.

BY THIS CROSS WE READ OUR FAM'LY BIBLE
PRAYER BY PRAYER.

(**TONIA** *joins them with* **SASHA**, *also bundled for travel. All move quietly, aware of the* **OFFICIALS** *who guard the stairs.*)

**TONIA**.
IN THIS ROOM I HAVE HELD MY HUSBAND.
IN THIS CHAIR I HAVE NURSED A SON.
IN THIS HOUSE MEMORIES SURROUND ME
ONE BY ONE.

**TONIA & ALEX**.
I WILL TOUCH YOU ONE MORE TIME.
I'LL BREATHE YOU IN,
AND TAKE YOU WITH ME.

**YURII**.
ON THESE SHELVES, THERE WILL STILL BE BOOKS.

**TONIA**.
IN THIS VASE, LILACS STILL WILL BLOOM.

**YURII, TONIA & ALEX**.
IN MY MIND, THIS HOUSE WILL LIVE WITHIN ME,
ROOM BY ROOM.

(**MARKEL** *enters holding a newspaper.*)

**MARKEL**.  The Reds killed them all, sir; the Tsar and his children massacred!

**ALEX**.  *(Taking the paper, with anguish.)* Dear God, that I should live to see such a day!

(*Enraged.*)

The White Army will hunt down these savages and drench their cursed Red Flag of revolution in their own treacherous blood!

**TONIA.** Is it all clear downstairs?

**MARKEL.** I gave the caretakers vodka. They're celebrating, can you imagine? This is the end of civilization, isn't it, Sir?

**TONIA.** Come, darling.

## Scene 1–13B: Streets of Moscow

*(As they hurry through the street, the* **FAMILY** *turns back to see their house one last time.)*

**YURII.**

IN MY HEART MOSCOW IS A YOUNG BOY,
BRIGHT WITH HOPE, EAGER EYES AGLEAM.

**YURII, TONIA & ALEX.**

LIVE IN ME, AND WE WILL BUILD A NEW LIFE
DREAM BY DREAM.

*(***YURII** *and his* **FAMILY** *are joined by* **OTHER FAMILIES** *fleeing Moscow.)*

**FAMILIES (JOINING GRADUALLY).**

IN THIS CHURCH, YOU AND I WERE MARRIED.
ON THESE TREES OUR CHILDREN USED TO CLIMB.
IN THIS SQUARE WE HEARD THE BELLS OF EASTER,
CHIME BY CHIME BY...

**FAMILIES.**

DOWN THESE LANES I WOULD GO TO MARKET.
IN THESE EAVES STARLINGS WOULD APPEAR.
THROUGH THE DAYS THE SEASONS TUMBLED BY US
SPRING BY SPRING, YEAR BY YEAR.

I WILL TOUCH YOU ONE MORE TIME,
I'LL BREATHE YOU IN AND TAKE YOU WITH ME...

*(***COMMUNISTS** *enter waving huge red banners, singing what has become an anthem. A train appears.)*

**COMMUNISTS.**

BLOOD ON THE SNOW,
THE BLOOD OF THE
  MARTYRS

**FAMILIES.**

DOWN THESE LANES
WE WOULD GO TO
  MARKET.

SPILLED FOR THE SAKE
OF A NEW WORLD WE
   MAKE!
COMRADE WORKERS
   UNITE
TO FIGHT IN A NEW WAY,

RED SUN AGLOW AT THE
DAWN OF A NEW DAY!

IN THESE EAVES
STARLINGS WOULD
   APPEAR.
THROUGH THE DAYS

THE SEASONS TUMBLED
   BY US
YEAR BY YEAR BY
YEAR.

(**FAMILIES** *board the crowded train.*
**COMMUNISTS** *wave red flags above.*)

PEACE AND BREAD
AND FREE LAND FOR
   EV'RYONE!
PEACE AND BREAD
AND FREE LAND FOR
   EV'RYONE!

IN MY HEART
MOSCOW IS A YOUNG BOY

BRIGHT WITH HOPE
EAGER EYES AGLEAM.

(*The train pulls out of the station, receding
into smoke as* **COMMUNISTS** *rally in the
foreground.*)

MASSES ARISE,
IN BONDAGE NO LONGER!

GROW EVER STRONGER!
THE SOUL OF A NATION
WE REDEEM!

LIVE IN ME,
AND WE WILL BUILD A
   NEW LIFE
DREAM BY DREAM
BY DREAM BY DREAM.
BY DREAM!

(**PASHA ANTIPOV** *is revealed in another
location, leading a contingent of renegade
* **PARTISANS**.*)

(**MARKEL** *stays behind, watching the train
depart as two worlds collide.*)

## End of Act One

# ACT TWO

## Scene 2–1: Farmland outside Yuriatin

### [MUSIC NO. 15 – WOMEN AND LITTLE CHILDREN / HE'S THERE]

### Projection Title: 1919 NEAR YURIATIN

*(***WOMEN*** work the earth for spring planting,* ***LARA*** *among them.)*

**WOMEN & LARA.**
NA NA, NA NARI
NA NA, NA NARI ...
SPRING IN THE URAL MOUNTAINS,
TAKE TO THE FIELD AND PLOW.
WOMEN AND LITTLE CHILDREN
DO ALL THE WORK NOW.
ALL OF THE MEN CONSCRIPTED,
OFF TO THE ENDLESS WAR.
WOMEN, CHILDREN
KEEP THE EARTH GROWING.
MEN DIE NOT KNOWING
WHAT THEY'RE DYING FOR!

*(An ***EARTHY WOMAN*** who will later play* ***KUBARIKHA***, steps forward, ploughing.)*

**EARTHY WOMAN (KUBARIKHA).**
BROTHERS KILLS BROTHER,

RED MURDERS WHITE.
NO ONE IN BED
TO BOTHER ME AT NIGHT.
NO ONE TO BEAT ME,
NO ONE TO DRINK AND WHORE.
LEAVE ME THE VODKA,
LET THEM GO TO WAR!

**WOMEN & LARA.**
AFTER THE SENSELESS FIGHT ENDS,
GOD ONLY PRAY IT DOES,
EV'RYTHING WILL GO BACK
TO THE WAY IT WAS
WITH MEN EITHER DEAD OR WOUNDED
MISSING AN ARM OR EYE.
WOMEN, CHILDREN
KEEP THE WORLD TURNING,
TOO BUSY EARNING DAILY BREAD TO CRY.
NA NA NA NA NA NA ...

> *(As the other* **WOMEN** *continue to work in the fields,* **YELENKA**, *a young townswoman, very upset, runs in looking for* **LARA**.*)*

**YELENKA.**  Soldiers took my Vasia! Rode off with him in broad daylight!

**LARA.**  Calm yourself, Yelenka. Which army were they, Whites or Reds?

**YELENKA.**  White Army, Red Army, who can tell anymore? They just dragged him from the yard. Not a word spoken. My poor Vasia – gone.

**LARA.**  No, Yelenka. He'll return. Never give up hope, and for now hold him safely in your heart.
LIKE SUNLIGHT IN THE WINTER CHILL,
HE'S THERE.
A SHADOW ON THE WINDOW SILL,

HE'S THERE.
A SONG HE SANG, A BOOK HE READ.
A LOOK HE GAVE, A WORD HE SAID
THAT STAYS FOREVER IN YOUR HEAD,
HE'S THERE.

*(The* **WOMEN** *take* **YELENKA** *to comfort her.*
**LARA** *stands apart, remembering* **YURII.***)*

ANOTHER DAY ALONE AND YET,
YOU'RE THERE.
AS VIVID AS THE DAY WE MET,
YOU'RE THERE.
THAT UNEXPECTED FLASH OF LIGHT
SHOCKS MY SOUL AND BURNS SO BRIGHT
AND STAYS WITH ME ALL THROUGH THE NIGHT,
YOU'RE THERE.
AND ALL AT ONCE I COME ALIVE,
A JOY I CAN'T EXPLAIN.
I FEEL YOU NEAR,
AND I HEAR YOU SOFTLY CALL MY NAME...
A CANDLE BURNS AND IN ITS GLOW,
YOU'RE THERE
IN PASSING TRAINS THAT COME AND GO,
YOU'RE THERE.
AS DAYS AND SEASONS TURN TO YEARS
IT'S YOUR HAND THAT DRIES MY TEARS.
WHEN I SIGH I KNOW YOU HEAR MY PRAYER.
WITH EV'RY BREATH OF AIR I BREATHE,
YOU'RE THERE.

*(***LARA** *rejoins the* **WOMEN** *and* **YELENKA** *as*
*they resume their work in the fields.)*

**SOME WOMEN.**
NA NA, NA NARI
NA NA, NA NARI NA!

**OTHER WOMEN.**
NA NA, NA NARI NARI
NA NA, NA NARI NA

**MOST WOMEN.**

SPRING IN THE URAL
MOUNTAINS,
GONE IS THE ICE AND
SNOW.
HARVEST WILL BE HERE
BEFORE YOU KNOW IT.
SOLDIERS TRAMPLE
MEADOWS.
WHO MAKES IT BLOOM
AGAIN?

**EARTHY WOMAN.**

NA NA, NA NARI NARI
NA NA, NA NARI NA!
NA NA, NA NARI NARI
NARI NARI NARI
NA NA, NA NARI NA!
NA NA, NA NARI NA!

**SOME WOMEN.**

WOMEN, CHILDREN,
WOMEN, CHILDREN

WOMEN, AND
LITTLE CHILDREN...

**OTHER WOMEN.**

WOMEN, CHILDREN,
WOMEN AND LITTLE
CHILDREN,
WOMEN,
CHILDREN...

*(An **OLD MAN** staggers past. The **PEASANT** **WOMAN** remarks ironically.)*

**EARTHY WOMAN (KUBARIKHA).**

AND A FEW OLD MEN.

**WOMEN.**

NA NA, NA NARI...

*(In the distance, a train whistle grows louder.)*

## Scene 2–2: Rail Depot in Yuriatin

*(The* **STATION-MASTER** *walks before the arriving train, ringing his bell. Several* **ARMED MEN** *stand near the rails.)*

**STATION MASTER.** Train from Moscow. Unauthorized personnel stay clear of the tracks. Train from Moscow arriving...

*(The train stops. The* **STATION MASTER** *lowers the stairs.* **YURII**, **SASHA**, **ALEX**, *and* **TONIA** *step down eyeing the deserted platform.)*

**YURII.** Didn't you wire ahead for the Caretaker to meet us here?

**TONIA.** Watch our belongings, we'll ask inside. Come Sasha, Papa...

**ALEX.** *(To* **SASHA**.*)* Stay close to me.

*(They wander off in search of information.* **THREE MEN**, *who were lingering on the tracks, approach* **YURII**; *one is* **CAPTAIN LIBERIUS**.*)*

**YURII.** Is there something you want?

**LIBERIUS.** Come with us nice and quiet, and you'll live to see the sun rise.

### [MUSIC NO. 15A – ARRIVAL AT YURIATIN]

*(They go. One* **PEASANT** *sees the "arrest."* **TONIA** *re-enters with* **ALEX** *and* **SASHA**.*)*

**ALEX.** *(To* **SASHA**, *handing him food.)* Take the rest of my apple, but make it last; we don't know when our next meal's coming.

*(***ALEX** *joins* **TONIA**. *She asks a* **PEASANT**.*)*

**TONIA.**  Excuse me, did you see a gentleman waiting here?

**STATION MASTER.**  *(Steps forward, speaking quietly.)* Strelnikov's men took him.

**TONIA.**  Strelnikov?

**PEASANT.**  Shhh, little sister, not so loud. Strelnikov hears everything – even the thoughts in your head.

**TONIA.**  What are you talking about? Who is *Strelnikov*?

**STATION MASTER.**  Commander of the Red Army Partisans. A man who makes Satan look like an angel of mercy.

**TONIA.**  But we're strangers here. He has no business with us.

**STATION MASTER.**  He needs no reason for what he does. He kills for pleasure – entire villages, old and young.

**TONIA.**  Where's the militia? They'd never allow such an outrage! Take me to this Strelnikov!

**PEASANT.**  Leave it, missus. No one gets near Strelnikov. Your best hope now is to pray.

> **(TONIA** *exits with* **PEASANT** *and* **STATION MASTER**. *The train revolves to become* **STRELNIKOV**'*s rail car headquarters.)*

## Scene 2–3: Strelnikov's Railway Car

### Projection Title: STRELNIKOV'S RAILCAR

(**STRELNIKOV**'s *back is to us.* **LIBERIUS** *and a* **PARTISAN** *bring* **YURII** *in.*)

**LIBERIUS**. We found him travelling east, Commander Strelnikov.

**STRELNIKOV**. Leave him.

(**STRELNIKOV** *turns: he is* **PASHA ANTIPOV**, *transformed, his face steely and cruel.* **LIBERIUS** *and the* **GUARD** *leave.*)

**YURII**. There must be a mistake. I arrived in the district mere hours ago.

**STRELNIKOV**. *(Imitating him.)* 'Oh, mere hours ago.' A Moscow aristocrat, by your accent. Imagine, two Muscovites crossing paths in this god-forsaken place.

**YURII**. *(Slightly curious.)* You're from Moscow?

**STRELNIKOV**. You have no idea who I am, do you?

**YURII**. How could I know anything about you?

**STRELNIKOV**. The same way I know everything about *you* at a glance: typical imperialist dog, assumes the world is his by right; property, wealth, women – never a thought that what he takes for himself might be someone else's loss.

**YURII**. *(Flaring up.)* Why do you Revolutionists always see the world in caricature: *I'm a White. You're a Red, a loyal Bolshevik*, on and on. But in the end, what difference does it make? We're all Russians, and in this civil war, every death is Russia's loss.

*(Remembers himself, falls silent.)*

Forgive me. The trip from Moscow was – tiring.

**STRELNIKOV**. *(Amused by* **YURII***'s petulant outburst.)* I'm called Strelnikov.

*(Extending a hand, which* **YURII** *shakes.)*

And if I'm not mistaken, I'm addressing the celebrated 'Doctor-poet,' Y.A. Zhivago.

**YURII**. You know who I am?

**STRELNIKOV**. Doesn't everyone? It's curious how so many of your kind end up dangling from a rope, but even so, a bourgeois parasite of your eminence – a Zhivago, no less – thinks he can simply board a train with his wife and family and flee to safety... completely unnoticed? We watch every train in and out of the district, Mister *Poet*. Well, sooner or later, everything we do catches up with us. Wouldn't you agree?

**YURII**. What do you want?

**STRELNIKOV**. I've heard inspiring reports of your service in the Great War.

**YURII**. I was a field-medic; I did nothing special.

**STRELNIKOV**. A field medic, yes, with the Tsar's Third Infanty Divison.

*(***YURII** *is surprised at the amount he knows.)*

A soldier from your division disappeared – his wife trained as a nurse and came to the front looking for him; perhaps you met her... Doctor. Larissa Antipova?

**YURII**. *(Excited but wary.)* Lara!

### [MUSIC NO. 16 – NO MERCY AT ALL]

Yes, of course I knew her; a wonderful nurse, everyone adored her. Did you by any chance know her husband? I've been told he didn't survive the war.

**STRELNIKOV**. Lara's husband died a very long time ago.

(**PARTISANS** *bring in a* **YOUNG PEASANT**.)

**PARTISAN GUARD**. This one was laying explosives on the tracks. He's been reporting every move we make to the Whites.

**YURII**. (*A plea to* **STRELNIKOV**.) Are you done with me?

**STRELNIKOV**. Don't you understand anything, Zhivago? It's over. Your life of privilege, your sentimental verse: it's over, it's the past! Now comes the reckoning.

**YURII**. Surely there's room in your revolution for an act of mercy.

**STRELNIKOV**. Blindfold him.

(**STRELNIKOV** *nods and* **PARTISANS** *lead him away, blindfolded.*)

**YOUNG PEASANT**. (*To* **STRELNIKOV**.) I didn't blow up your train, Strelnikov; I swear, by Saint Sebastian, I'm innocent.

(**STRELNIKOV** *cuts him off coldly, watching* **YURII** *outside as he sings.*)

**STRELNIKOV**.
MEN OF YOUR KIND,
TRAITORS LIKE YOU
TALK ABOUT MERCY
BUT WHAT DID YOU DO    **YOUNG PEASANT**.
WHEN THE POWER WAS    I did nothing!
   YOURS?
DID YOU PROTEST?
OR DID YOU JUST CLOSE
YOUR EYES LIKE THE REST...?

**YOUNG PEASANT**. Close my eyes?

**STRELNIKOV.**

> WELL, THE TABLES HAVE TURNED.
>
> I'M IN COMMAND.
>
> DOCTORS AND LAWYERS
>
> AND POETS BE DAMNED.
>
> ALL YOU PRIVILEGED MEN,
>
> POMPOUS AND WISE
>
> PUFFING CIGARS ON A MOUNTAIN OF LIES
>
> BUT THE TRUTH CRIES OUT TO BE TOLD
>
> FOR A NEW WORLD,
>
> EV'RYTHING OLD HAS TO FALL.
>
> NO MERCY AT ALL.

**YOUNG PEASANT.**  But I'm a farmer. I hate the Whites as much as you!

**STRELNIKOV.**

> JUSTICE IS DEAD.
>
> LIFE ISN'T FAIR.
>
> YOUR BRAND OF JUSTICE
>
> BROUGHT ONLY DESPAIR      **YOUNG PEASANT.**
>
> TO AN INNOCENT GIRL,               What girl?
>
> VICTIM OF LUST,
>
> USED FOR AMUSEMENT
>
> THEN TOSSED IN THE DUST.
>
> AND THERE IS NO JUSTICE FOR SWINE
>
> TILL YOUR WHOLE CLASS
>
> DIES IN A LINE AT THE WALL!
>
> NO MERCY AT ALL!

**YOUNG PEASANT.**  Sir, you have the wrong man –!

**STRELNIKOV.**

> HOW MANY NIGHTS
>
> HAVE I DREAMED OF THIS DAY,
>
> ACHING TO EVEN THE SCORE.
>
> MEN OF YOUR KIND
>
> GAVE HER CHOC'LATES AND BRANDY,

BUT I GAVE HER A WAR!
ALL I HAVE TO DO IS AIM THE GUN.
ALL I HAVE TO SAY... IS WHEN.
PURGE YOU ONE BY ONE,
AND WHEN I AM DONE
RUSSIA WILL BE PURE AGAIN...

(**LIBERIUS** *enters the railcar.*)

**LIBERIUS.** What do we do with the prisoner?

(**STRELNIKOV** *doesn't answer.*)

Commander?

**STRELNIKOV.** I heard you! He's mine now. What's the rush? Let him go.

(**LIBERIUS** *starts towards the* **YOUNG PEASANT**.)

Not *him.*

(**LIBERIUS** *nods, goes out to issue order.*)

**LIBERIUS.** Release the prisoner.

(*A* **PARTISAN GUARD** *brushes in past* **YURII** *exiting.* **TONIA** *has entered, frantic.*)

**TONIA.** Yurii! Yurii!

**PARTISAN GUARD.** This woman says she's the prisoner's wife.

**STRELNIKOV.** (*Knowingly.*) The wife, too! Very good.

(**YURII** *and* **TONIA** *exit.* **STRENIKOV**'s *eyes follow* **YURII**.)

MERCY YOU PLEAD.
MERCY YOU'LL GET.
I'LL BE HERE WAITING

AND WATCHING YOU SWEAT
LIKE A RAT IN A CAGE,
CRINGING IN DREAD,
CORNERED LIKE ME
WHEN THE GUTTER RAN RED

AND THE STEEL BLADES
TORE THROUGH OUR SKIN
AS THE TSAR'S GUARD
BELLOWED ITS INFAMOUS CALL
NOW REAP WHAT YOU SOW
"NO MERCY AT ALL!"

(**STRELNIKOV** *coolly fires a bullet into the* **PEASANT***'s head and orders* **LIBERIUS***:*)

Throw him in the ravine.

**[MUSIC NO. 16A – NO MERCY (PLAYOFF)]**

## Scene 2–4: Road to the Kruger Estate

(**YURII** *and* **TONIA** *argue along a country road.*)

**TONIA**. Who is this man Strelnikov? Everyone here is terrified of him.

**YURII**. He has a private army, fanatical Reds. They call themselves *Partisans*.

**TONIA**. What did they want with you?

**YURII**. It was a misunderstanding. There's nothing to worry about.

**TONIA**. You were right about this place. We should never have come. Every day there's someone new in power. It's more confusing than Moscow ever was and we've no friends here we can trust.

**YURII**. Tonia, calm yourself, *please*! The civil war's everywhere in Russia. We're as safe here as anywhere. We'll lie low. No one will even know we're here.

(**YURII** *and* **TONIA** *cross back into the Cottage at the Kruger Estate.*)

## Scene 2-5: Library at Yuriatin

(**LARA** *and* **YELENKA** *lock up the library after work.*

**YELENKA.** If I could trust anyone else to close up the library, you know I wouldn't ask you. Are you angry with me, Lara? Is it too soon after losing my Vasia to behave like this?

**LARA.** Go meet your Mystery Gentleman, Yelenka. No one can mourn forever.

**YELENKA.** I've never even laid eyes on him, but look at his penmanship...

(*Shows the note.*)

...he does loops! 'Dearest temptress Yelenka; Librarian of my heart.' 'Temptress Yelenka!' Me! I know it's wrong to think this way, but I'm not the only one who's noticed that since gentlemen started fleeing here from Moscow, the town is a lot more interesting. Didn't you live in Moscow once?

## [MUSIC NO. 16B – YELINKA'S LETTER / IN THIS HOUSE (REPRISE)]

Are they all so forward in the big cities?

(**LARA** *is rapt in her own thoughts.*)

Lara?

**LARA.** I'm sorry, what did you say?

**YELENKA.** You still miss him so much?

**LARA.** (*Slightly sharp.*) Miss who?

**YELENKA.** Your husband. Pasha.

**LARA.** (*Relaxing.*) Of course I do.

*(To herself.)*

I miss him... all the time.

*(**YELENKA** leaves **LARA** staring into the distance, and we go to:)*

## Scene 2–6: Cottage and Grounds of the Kruger Estate

> (**ALEX** *walks the path to the estate with* **SASHA**. **YURII** *and* **TONIA** *sit inside,* **YURII** *drinking tea.*)

**ALEX**.
ON THIS LAWN,
I REMEMBER PICNICS.
DOWN THIS PATH,
NANA'S GARDEN GREW.
BY THIS BROOK,
THE WILLOW TREES WOULD WHISPER
ALL NIGHT THROUGH.
IN THAT ROOM,
YOUR MAMA TOOK HER FIRST STEPS.
MAIDS PREPARED
TEA WITH HONEYCOMB.
NOW WE LIVE
IN THE CARETAKER'S COTTAGE...

> (**ALEX**, **TONIA**, **SASHA**, *and* **YURII** *sit in the cottage while* **ALEX** *opens a novel.*)

Is everyone comfortable?

**TONIA**.  We're fine, Papa. Read.

**SASHA**.  Can I have a turn, Grandpapa. Just the first page?

> (**ALEX** *looks to* **YURII** *&* **TONIA** *for permission, then hands him the book.*)

**ALEX**.  Pronounce each word clearly; my hearing's not what it was.

**SASHA**.  *(Reading.)* 'Chapter One: All happy families are alike; but every unhappy family is unhappy in its own way.' We read this already.

**ALEX.** We've read every book in the cottage, and now we'll read them all again.

**SASHA.** Why can't we go to town and get new books from the library?

**YURII.** *(Preoccupied, sharp.)* Sasha, that's enough; read!

**ALEX.** *(Off* **TONIA***'s look.)* I think it's someone's bedtime. Come, young man, I'll tuck you in and we'll pretend we live up the hill in the Kruger Mansion, and you have your own bed in your own room, and this cramped little cottage is all just a bad dream.

*(***ALEX*** takes* **SASHA** *to bed.)*

**TONIA.** How long are you going to keep putting it off, Yurochka?

**YURII.** I've put nothing off.

**TONIA.** First you had to fix the roof. Then you had to plant the garden. Now the fence needs repair. Go to town, find a quiet corner of the library, and *write.*

**YURII.** Other work comes first.

**TONIA.** Nothing comes before your verse. We fled Moscow for peace of mind. No one's troubling us here. It's time to be selfish, and follow your heart.

**YURII.** My heart is here... with my family.

**TONIA.** Don't argue. Tomorrow, you'll leave for town first thing in the morning.

*(The scene transitions: as* **TONIA** *leaves,* **LARA** *appears across the stage, closing the library.* **YURII** *rises and turns towards her on...)*

## Scene 2–7: A Street past the Library in Yuriatin

**YURII**. Lara?

**LARA**. *(Half to herself.)* Oh dear God if I turn and you're not there…!

### [MUSIC NO. 17 – LOVE FINDS YOU]

*(She turns, and with disbelief, they approach more and more rapidly as they accept that this is finally happening. Their embrace is hasty, awkward and passionate. Breathlessly, they hold each other.)*

**YURII**. I tried to stay away!

**LARA**. It's been torture knowing you were so near and wouldn't come to see me.

**YURII**. You knew!

**LARA**. *(Nearly laughing with joy.)* A celebrated poet from Moscow hiding on the Kruger Estate? Of course I knew.

**YURII**. I thought I'd be lost if I saw you. Forgive me.

**LARA**. Forgive you? All that's made my life bearable is the hope that I might catch a glimpse of you, just riding past in the distance.

**YURII**. Lara!

*(They finally kiss hungrily.)*

**LARA**. Stop. It's too dangerous. If Strelnikov finds out…

**YURII**. The Partisan commander? Why would he care?

**LARA**. He's my husband. Or *was* when he was called Pasha Antipov.

**YURII**. Your husband's alive? God help me, I was his prisoner. He asked about you.

**LARA**.  His spies are everywhere. No one in the village moves without his knowing. He's like an angry child with an army at his command, keeping watch over me day and night.

**YURII**.  Are you afraid?

**LARA**.  Aren't you?

**YURII**.  I'm done with fear – I've been afraid of my own thoughts, afraid to let them go where they will because they always return to you...

*(Yielding to their feelings, they kiss.)*

ALL THE MIDNIGHTS FILLED WITH LONGING.
ALL THE HUNGER, ALL THE TEARS,
ALWAYS SEARCHING FOR THIS MOMENT
AS THE MOMENTS TURNED TO YEARS.

**LARA**.

DIDN'T KNOW WHY I WAS WAITING
BUT NOW IN YOUR ARMS I DO.
YOU CAN LOOK, BUT YOU DON'T FIND LOVE.
LOVE FINDS YOU.
NEVER WHEN YOU ASK,
NEVER WHEN YOU GUESS,
SUDDENLY A RUSH OF HAPPINESS.

**YURII**.

SLIPPING THROUGH THE DOOR, SILENT AS A PRAYER.
ALMOST LIKE IT ALWAYS HAD BEEN THERE.

*(They mount the stairs to **LARA**'s apartment.)*

**LARA & YURII**.

HOW ASTOUNDING YET HOW SIMPLE
ALL THE TIME I NEVER KNEW
THAT THE TRUTH IS YOU DON'T FIND LOVE.
LOVE FINDS YOU.

## Scene 2–7B: Multiple Locations: Komarovsky's Desk – Moscow

(**KOMAROVSKY**, *in an official's uniform with a red armband, studies paperwork.*)

**KOMAROVSKY.**
IN A TIME OF CHANGE
ONE MUST RE-ADAPT,
LEAVING ANCIENT HISTORY BEHIND.
OUTWARDLY I THRIVE.
INWARDLY I'M TRAPPED.
HAUNTED BY A SHADOW IN MY MIND...
DIDN'T WANT IT. DIDN'T NEED IT.
ALL THE SAME, THE FEELING GREW.
IT'S A GODDAMN INCONVENIENCE
WHEN LOVE FINDS YOU!

## Split Scene: Strelnikov's Railcar Headquarters

(**STRELNIKOV** *appears with binoculars.*)

**LIBERIUS.** Commander Strelnikov, I've lost a third of my men to typhoid fever. We need medical help.

**STRELNIKOV.** All my commanders need something, *Captain* Liberius. Wait your turn.

**LIBERIUS.** Yes, sir.

(*He exits.*)

**STRELNIKOV.**
A SOLDIER NEEDS TO FIGHT UNTIL THE WAR IS DONE,
PUSH ASIDE THE PERSONAL TILL EV'RY BATTLE'S WON.
ENEMIES TO INFILTRATE, CHALLENGES TO SOLVE.
NOT PERMITTING SENTIMENT TO WEAKEN HIS
    RESOLVE ...!

**KOMAROVSKY, STRELNIKOV & YURII** (*Variously.*)
BUT I HEAR HER IN THE SILENCE
AND I FEEL HER IN THE AIR,

AND I SEE HER COMING TOWARDS ME
WITH THE SUNLIGHT IN HER HAIR.

**STRELNIKOV.**
EV'RY MEM'RY IS A DAGGER

**KOMAROVSKY.**
AND THE BLADE KEEPS PIERCING THROUGH,

**KOMAROVSKY & STRELNIKOV.**
FOR NO MATTER WHERE YOU'RE HIDING...
LOVE FINDS YOU.

(**TONIA** *enters the cottage. She is in very dim light.*)

**TONIA.**
> PEOPLE THINK THEY 'CHOOSE.'
> THEY DON'T HAVE A CHOICE.
> SOMETHING OVERWHELMING TAKES CONTROL.
> FEAR OF WHAT YOU'LL LOSE
> SILENCES YOUR VOICE.
> THERE'S A SECRET HIDING IN YOUR SOUL...

**KOMAROVSKY & STRELNIKOV.**
> THERE'S A SECRET HIDING...

**LARA & YURII.**
> AND IT THRILLS YOU

*(All following lines overlapping.)*

**LARA.**
> AND IT HAUNTS YOU.
> AND ALL THE TIME YOU'RE ALL ALONE
> I NEVER KNEW
> LOVE ALWAYS COMES IN AN INSTANT
> WHEN IT CHOOSES

**TONIA.**
> AND NOW IT HAUNTS YOU.
> AND ALL THE TIME YOU'RE SO ALONE
> I NEVER KNEW
> IT CAN SEIZE YOU IN AN INSTANT
> ANY TIME

**YURII.**
> AND IT THRILLS YOU
> IT GETS BETTER
> AND AT TIMES IT TAUNTS YOU.
> IT'S A BLESSING, IT'S A CURSE.
> IT CAN SEIZE YOU IN AN INSTANT
> ANY TIME IT CHOOSES TO

**STRELNIKOV.**

AND IT HAUNTS YOU,
IT GETS BETTER
AS IT TAUNTS YOU
AND IT'S A CURSE.
IT CAN SEIZE YOU IN AN INSTANT
ANY TIME IT CHOOSES TO

**KOMAROVSKY.**

IT GETS WORSE.
IT FORGIVES YOU AS IT TAUNTS YOU
IT'S A CURSE.
IT CAN SEIZE YOU IN AN INSTANT
ANY TIME IT CHOOSES TO

| **YURII, TONIA, STRELNIKOV & KOMAROVSKY** | **LARA** |
|---|---|
| BUT IT OWNS YOU FOR A LIFETIME | BUT IT'S FOR A LIFETIME |

**ALL.**

WHEN LOVE FINDS YOU!

## [MUSIC NO. 17A – LOVE FINDS YOU (REPRISE)]

**LARA.** Come earlier next week. I took the afternoon off.

**YURII.** Next week won't be possible.

*(Pained.)*

Lara...

**LARA.** Don't! I prayed you'd find a way to forget everything when we're together and enjoy the same happiness I feel.

**YURII.** I do... when we're together. But then I have to leave, and my other life is always waiting.

**LARA.**  Then this is the time we were given. And it's over. And we must be grateful.

**YURII.**  I wonder – Is it better never to know happiness like this is possible?

**LARA.**  I'd live my whole life again for this little time with you.

**YURII.**  But you *deserve* more. And so does she. She feels the distance between us, and it breaks my heart. Then I come to you and feel that everything in the world is alive and full of promise.

**LARA.**  Shhh, no more Yurii Andreyevich. We both knew from the start that it had to end.

**YURII.**  I'll send someone for the books I need. It's best I avoid the library; you understand.

**LARA.**  Yes.

**YURII.**  This is the end, Lara, you must believe that. Tell me you know it's true.

**LARA.**  No.

> (**YURII** *can think of no way to change her mind. She forces herself to leave. He watches her go.*)

NO, THERE'S NOTHING YOU CAN DO
WITH THE HEARTACHE AND THE LONGING
WHEN LOVE... FINDS...

> (*She goes indoors, overwhelmed.* **YELENKA** *enters with* **LIBERIUS** *and* **PARTISAN GUARDS.**)

**YELENKA.**  (*Identifying the departing* **YURII**.) There he is!

**LIBERIUS.**  (*Blocking* **YURII**.) Some of my men need a doctor.

**YURII.** Tell me where, and I'll come first thing in the morning.

**LIBERIUS.** You see the moon, doctor? Our camp is just that far away. And like the moon, it keeps moving around. You'll never find us without an escort.

(*He nods to his men to take* **YURII** *away.*)

**YURII.** But... my family's expecting me. My equipment's at home...

(*They take* **YURII** *away.* **STRELNIKOV** *steps from shadows.* **LIBERIUS** *hands* **YELENKA** *money, she exits.* **STRELNIKOV** *watches* **LARA***'s window.*)

**STRELNIKOV.** You asked for a doctor, I give you a doctor. Treat him well. If he comes to harm, you won't get another.

**LIBERIUS.** Yes, sir.

**STRELNIKOV.** Keep him far away from here.

(**STRELNIKOV** *exits.* **LIBERIUS** *watches him.*)

## Scene 2–8: The Partisan Camp

### Projection Title: 1920 – CIVIL WAR

### [MUSIC NO. 18 – NOWHERE TO HIDE]

*(The stage fills with* **PARTISANS** *breaking camp; some throw corpses in a fire pit. Terrified captive* **WOMEN** *scream.* **YOUNG PARTISANS** *sit calmly eating rotten food amidst the carnage.)*

**PARTISANS.**
> WHEREVER YOU RUN,
> THERE'S NOWHERE TO HIDE.
> THE MOUNTAIN IS STEEP.
> THE RIVER IS WIDE.
> THE TRACKS ARE DESTROYED.
> THERE'S NO TRAIN TO RIDE.

**LIBERIUS.**
> SO MAKE UP YOUR MIND.
> YOU BETTER DECIDE
> WHICH SIDE YOU'RE FIGHTING FOR.

**PARTISANS.**
> WHEREVER YOU RUN,
> THERE'S NOWHERE TO HIDE.
> THE GRAVEYARDS ARE FILLED
> WITH TRAITORS WHO TRIED.
> SO SLEEP WITH THE BONES
> OF DEVILS WHO DIED.

**LIBERIUS.**
> YOU GIVE UP YOUR SOUL,
> YOU FORFEIT YOUR PRIDE

AND DIRT IS ALL YOU'RE WORTH...

**LIBERIUS & PARTISANS.**
TILL THE LAST WHITE DOG
IS WIPED OFF THE FACE OF THE EARTH!

**LIBERIUS.** *(Issuing general orders.)* We move camp at midnight. Burn what you can't carry. Leave the wounded.

*(***TWO PARTISANS*** enter with a ***COMRADE*** on a stretcher-filthy, weak, mouth clotted with blood.)*

**PARTISAN.** One of ours, Sir. The White Army took his tongue, but they got no information with it.

**YURII.** He needs morphine, twenty milligrams.

**LIBERIUS.** *(Intercepting the syringe.)* I'll take that. No point wasting medicine on a dead man.

**YURII.** For pity's sake, why bring me here if I can't do my job? That morphine's for the wounded.

**LIBERIUS.** Comrade Doctor, it's upsetting when you bark at me like an angry dog. Aren't we friends?

**YURII.** Lay off that poison long enough, and it might sink in; I'm your prisoner, your captive. I want no part of this nightmare. I want to be home with – those I love.

**LIBERIUS.** But you and me, we're like family. I share dinner with you in my tent. We have elevated conversations about philosophy and art. Surely, you'd miss me, Doctor.

**PARTISANS.**
WE KNOW THIS TERRAIN
AS YOU NEVER WILL!
THE FORK IN THE ROAD,
THE RIDGE ON THE HILL.

**LIBERIUS.**

NO GOVERNMENT WORKS.
NO GOD WILL PROVIDE.
WHEN ANARCHY RULES,
THERE'S NOWHERE TO HIDE!

**PARTISANS.**
THERE'S NOWHERE TO HIDE!
NOWHERE TO HIDE...!

> (**YURII** *looks in the direction of Yuriatin, wondering, and we see...*)

## Scene 2-9: The Library, Yuriatin

*(The Library in Yuriatin has bookshelves, a small desk, a reading table, benches.* **TONIA** *is at the library door with* **SASHA**. *Inside,* **LARA** *is on duty; only a few readers present.)*

**SASHA.** Mama, you said it's dangerous to be seen in town.

**TONIA.** Shh.

*(Barely thinking.)*

We mustn't talk in the library...

*(They enter and approach* **LARA** *at the desk. Readers show scant interest.)*

I'm looking for a book of verse. 'Searching through the Rain.'

**LARA.** I'm afraid everyone's looking. There's a waiting list for months.

*(With pride.)*

Russia's hungry for every word the author writes.

**TONIA.** I'm his wife.

**LARA.** *(A brief hesitation.)* I think I have one copy left.

**TONIA.** He came here often to write. Perhaps you met him?

**LARA.** I'm – rarely on call. I teach at the middle school.

**TONIA.** The regular librarian's called Yelenka; I know.

**LARA.** You *know* Yelenka?

**TONIA.** She visited me. There were things she thought I should know.

## [MUSIC NO. 19 – IT COMES AS NO SURPRISE]

**LARA**. *(Understanding instantly.)* I see. And this would be his son?

**TONIA**. *Our* son, yes...

**SASHA**. *(To **LARA**.)* Do you have a book about flying machines?

　　*(**TONIA** becomes possessive.)*

**TONIA**. Come with me, Sasha.

　　*(She finds **SASHA** a book to read, seats him at a table, then returns to **LARA**.)*

We haven't heard a word since he disappeared.

**LARA**. *(Wanting to say more.)* I'm very sorry.

**TONIA**. Thank you...

　　*(**TONIA** and **LARA** each sing their private thoughts, unheard by the other one.)*

HERE WE ARE, FACE TO FACE.
NOW MY HEART BEGINS TO RACE
SUDDENLY THERE'S NO ESCAPE
FROM WHAT I'M FEELING

**LARA**.
ALL AT ODDS.

**TONIA**.
SHY AND SCARED.

**LARA**.
LOST FOR WORDS.

**TONIA**.

UNPREPARED.

**BOTH.**

AN ANGUISH THAT I DARE NOT RISK REVEALING...

**LARA.**

BUT IT COMES AS NO SURPRISE

**TONIA.**

SHE IS GRACIOUS.

**LARA.**

SHE IS KIND.

**BOTH.**

MORE THAN I WOULD BE
IF I WERE IN HER PLACE.

**TONIA.**

WHEN I DREAMED ABOUT THIS DAY
I WAS SURE OF WHAT I'D SAY

**BOTH.**

BUT IT'S NOT AT ALL
THE WAY THAT I IMAGINED, FACE TO FACE.

*(**LARA** approaches **TONIA** at the shelves and finds her the book she's looking for.)*

**LARA.** Why don't you keep this.

**TONIA.**

HAS SHE HEARD WHERE HE IS?

**LARA.**

IF HE'S HURT?

**TONIA.**

IF HE LIVES?

**BOTH.**

I PRAY MY DARKEST FEAR ISN'T SHOWING.
SO THE WORDS STAY INSIDE.

**LARA.**

LIKE MY HOPE.

**TONIA.**

LIKE MY PRIDE.

**BOTH.**

AM I MORE AFRAID
OF ASKING HER OR KNOWING?
BUT IT COMES AS NO SURPRISE

**TONIA.**

SHE'S HIS PASSION.

**LARA.**

SHE'S HIS WIFE.

**BOTH.**

AND I KNOW I COULD NEVER INTERFERE.
AND A LITTLE OF ME DIES
WHEN I LOOK INTO HER EYES.

**TONIA.**

IS IT ANGER?

**LARA.**

IS IT SADNESS?

**BOTH.**

IS IT MADNESS
THAT BRINGS US HERE?

**LARA.**

SHOULDN'T I BE CALM AND DISTANT?

**TONIA.**

SHOULDN'T I BE COLD AND PROUD?

**BOTH.**

I KNOW THAT IT'S THE WISER THING
TO STAY RESTRAINED,
BUT STILL I WANT TO SPEAK.

> STILL I WANT TO SCREAM.
> STILL I WANT TO CRY OUT LOUD...!
> AND IT COMES AS NO SURPRISE

**LARA.**

> THERE'S FORGIVENESS IN HER EYES.

**BOTH.**

> AND IT'S TAKING ALL MY STRENGTH
> TO HIDE THE TEARS.

**LARA.**                    **TONIA.**

> AND IT COMES AS
>     NO SURPRISE           AND IT COMES AS
> THAT HE NEEDS HER IN       NO SURPRISE
>     HIS LIFE ...

**LARA.**

> BUT IT COMES AS A SURPRISE

**BOTH.**

> I FEEL HIM CLOSER WHEN *SHE* IS NEAR...

> *(They stand next to each other, reading together from the book of* **YURII**'s *poetry.)*

> I FEEL HIM CLOSER... WHEN SHE IS NEAR.

## Scene 2–10: Secluded Area of the Partisan Camp

### Projection Title: 1921 – SIBERIA

### [MUSIC NO. 19A – KUBARIKHI]

(**PARTISANS** *hurry back and forth in the shadowy woods.* **TWO PARTISANS** *shove* **KUBARIKHA** *on, a wild-looking peasant woman, filthy and blood-stained.*)

**PARTISANS.** *(Variously.)*

NOWHERE TO RUN.

NOWHERE TO HIDE.

NOWHERE TO RUN.

NOWHERE...

**PARTISAN ONE.** Sit quiet, auntie. No more trouble from you.

(**LIBERIUS** *enters with* **YURII**, *who has a beard now, and shrunken eyes.*)

**LIBERIUS.** We know she's been spying for the Whites, but when we tighten the screws, she puts on a crazy act.

**YURII.** If she won't talk under torture, what do you expect me to do?

**LIBERIUS.** You're a doctor. See if she knows which end is up. We need names, troop movements, anything the Whites are planning.

**YURII.** I can't interrogate a prisoner. I'm a prisoner myself.

**LIBERIUS.** Prisoner? My friend, you've been free to stroll off into the woods anytime you like. You're here because *you chose it*. Better than all the complications back home, huh? That's the beauty of war. Am I right, doctor?

**YURII**. *(After a moment's hesitation.)* Can I be alone with her?

**PARTISAN TWO**. Careful, Doctor; she's strong as an ox and violent.

> (**LIBERIUS** *and the* **TWO PARTISANS** *back away.* **YURII** *approaches* **KUBARIKHA**.)

**YURII**. Don't be afraid, auntie. I'm a doctor, I won't hurt you.

> (**YURII** *sits beside* **KUBARIKHA**. *She pulls back.* **YURII** *notices an object in her hand.*)

What's that you're holding?

**KUBARIKHA**. *(Opening her hand reluctantly.)* A toy for Kolya, my youngest.

**YURII**. *(Impressed.)* A reindeer.

**KUBARIKHA**. *(Proud.)* My husband can carve any animal – rabbit, fish, even once an elephant.

**YURII**. *(Examines it.)* It's beautifully made. Where *is* your family?

**KUBARIKHA**. *(Cryptic.)* They're all safe in the woods, waiting for me to join them.

**YURII**. Let's pray that it can happen soon.

**KUBARIKHA**. Oh, it will, Doctor – right now.

> (**YURII** *doesn't see her pull out his knife from his coat pocket until it's too late. With a quick motion she cuts open her neck and falls sideways.*)

**YURII**. Dear God, no...!

> *(He puts pressure on her neck artery.)*

Someone help me!!

*(LIBERIUS hurries in with PARTISANS.)*

She's choking on her own blood!

**LIBERIUS.** *(To the YOUNG PARTISAN.)* Shoot her.

*(The YOUNG PARTISAN, overcome, can't pull the trigger. KUBARIKHA writhes on the ground.)*

**YURII.** Hurry, for God's sake, don't let her suffer!

*(Unable to watch her suffer, YURII grabs the PARTISAN's pistol and shoots KUBARIKHA.)*

**LIBERIUS.** *(Beaming.)* There, now you're one of us!!!

## [MUSIC NO. 20 – ASHES AND TEARS]

*(KUBARIKHA, dead, is dragged off by TWO PARTISANS. Lights on YURII who begins to awaken from his nightmare.)*

**YURII.** No. I am not one of you.

I AM YURII ANDREYEVICH ZHIVAGO!
I WILL NOT LEAVE A LEGACY OF SHAME.

*(As the music swells, he quickly packs his few belongings in a bag, including KUBARIKHA's carved animal, and begins his long trek home.)*

HEART KEEP BEATING, KEEP BEATING
DON'T LET ME DOWN.
JUST LET MY FEET KEEP MOVING, KEEP MOVING.
DON'T LET ME FOUNDER.
AFTER ALL MY WAITING,
THROUGH ALL THE WASTED YEARS,
WILL I FIND MY LIFE
OR ONLY ASHES AND TEARS?
ONLY ASHES, ASHES AND TEARS?

*(A whistle alerts **PARTISANS** that **YURII** has escaped. They pursue him. Dodging the **PARTISANS'** flashlight beams, **YURII** jumps into a trench and hides there to escape them.)*

**LIBERIUS & PARTISANS.**
WHEREVER YOU TURN
THERE'S NOWHERE TO HIDE!
THE GRAVEYARDS ARE FILLED
WITH TRAITORS WHO TRIED!
THE TRACKS IN THE SNOW
WILL ACT AS A GUIDE.
WHEREVER YOU RUN
THERE'S NOWHERE TO HIDE!

*(**YURII** emerges from the trenches, still hiding from the **PARTISANS**. A train appears filled with **WOMEN WAR REFUGEES**.)*

**YURII.**
LUNGS KEEP BREATHING,
KEEP BREATHING,
STEADY AND SLOW.
JUST HELP MY BLOOD
    KEEP PUMPING,
KEEP PUMPING.
I MUST KEEP GOING.
DARKENED CLOUDS

| | |
|---|---|
| AND BURNED OUT TOWNS | **WOMEN.** |
| AROUSE MY DEEPEST FEARS. | AH |
| LORD, I PRAY YOU LEAVE ME | AH |
| MORE THAN ASHES AND TEARS, | AH |
| MORE THAN ASHES, ASHES AND TEARS. | AH |

(**YURII** *climbs aboard the train and hides among the* **WOMEN REFUGEES.** *The* **PARTISANS** *continue to give chase.* **ONE WOMAN** *helps disguise* **YURII** *with a shawl.*)

**LIBERIUS & PARTISANS.**
WE KNOW THIS TERRAIN

**THREE BASSES.**
WE KNOW THIS TERRAIN

**LIBERIUS & PARTISANS.**
AS YOU NEVER WILL!

**THREE BASSES.**
AS YOU NEVER WILL!

**LIBERIUS & PARTISANS.**
THE FORK IN THE ROAD,

**THREE BASSES.**
THE FORK IN THE ROAD,

**LIBERIUS & PARTISANS.**
THE RIDGE ON THE HILL!

**THREE BASSES.**
THE RIDGE ON THE HILL!

**LIBERIUS & PARTISANS.**
WE'LL SCOUR THE WOODS

**LIBERIUS, PARTISANS & THREE BASSES.**
YOU COWER INSIDE.
THERE'S NOWHERE TO RUN
AND NOWHERE TO HIDE!

| **YURII.** | **LIBERIUS & PARTISANS.** |
|---|---|
| HEART KEEP BEATING. | NOWHERE TO RUN AWAY! |
| KEEP BEATING. | YOU WOULDN'T LAST A DAY! |
| DON'T LET ME DOWN. | LOST IN A MAZE OF TREES, |

JUST LET MY

FEET KEEP MOVING,
KEEP MOVING.
DON'T LET ME FOUNDER.
AFTER ALL MY WAITING,
THROUGH ALL THE
   WASTED YEARS,
WILL I FIND MY LIFE
OR ONLY ASHES
   AND TEARS?

ONLY ASHES,
   ASHES AND TEARS.

HOW LONG BEFORE YOU
   FREEZE?
NO ROOF TO SHELTER YOU
NO ROAD TO COVER YOUR
TRACKS IN THE SNOW.
WE KNOW WHERE YOU GO.
THERE IS NO BREAKING
   FREE FROM US.
NOWHERE TO RUN AWAY!
YOU WOULDN'T LAST A DAY!
WE FIND THE TRAIL
   BEHIND YOU.
ASHES AND THE
   FOOTPRINTS OF YOUR.... .

*(The* **REFUGEES** *vanish with the train as* **YURII** *leaps off.)*

*(Abstractly, the* **PARTISANS** *return, magnified in* **YURII***'s mind – he's exhausted, losing his grasp.)*

*(The wall of* **PARTISANS** *'pushes'* **YURII** *back. They shine their flashlights at him and the audience as he tries to run for cover.)*

**LIBERIUS & PARTISANS.** *(Variously.)*
   THE FARTHER YOU RUN,
   THE HARDER YOU FALL!
   THERE'S NOWHERE TO FLEE,
   NO PLACE YOU CAN CRAWL!
   WITH ICE IN YOUR VEINS
   AND EYES GOING BLIND,
   WE'RE ONE STEP AHEAD
   AND ONE STEP AHEAD.
   ONE STEP AHEAD
   AND ONE STEP AHEAD.
   ONE STEP AHEAD

AND ONE STEP AHEAD.
ONE STEP AHEAD
AND ONE STEP AHEAD.
ONE STEP AHEAD
AND ONE STEP AHEAD.
ONE STEP AHEAD
AND ONE STEP AHEAD ...!

(The **PARTISANS** march forward.)

(Exhausted, **YURII** looks up through the black night and is amazed to see **LARA**, bathed in an aura of gold, the light of the midnight winter sun.)

(The **PARTISANS** vanish.)

**LARA**.  Yurii!

## [MUSIC NO. 20A – ICE PALACE]

(**LARA** comes forward, reaching him just as **YURII** collapses into her arms. Scene transitions to...)

## Scene 2–11: Abandoned Kruger Mansion: The "Ice Palace"

### Projection Title: THE OLD KRUGER MANSION

(**YURII** *lies under a blanket.*)

**LARA**. Rest my love. You're safe here.

(**YURII** *makes a sound.* **LARA** *leans closer, takes his hand.*)

What do you need? Hold my hand, take my strength.

(**YURII** *props himself up, lost. He is gaunt and weak.*)

**YURII**. Where am I?

(*Focusing.*)

Lara!

**LARA**. You've been unconscious for days. I thought I'd lost you.

**YURII**. Where's my family? Where's Tonia?

**LARA**. They fled. The Partisans are in control of Yuriatin. They're killing anyone without calloused hands.

**YURII**. I have to find out if they're alive.

**LARA**. Strelnikov let them escape. I sent him word through channels... the only favor I'll ever ask him; to spare your family. But I – couldn't leave.

(*She hands him an envelope.*)

This came from Moscow.

(**YURII** *opens the envelope and reads the letter.* **TONIA** *appears in a spot, dressed in traveling* *and carrying a valise.* **SASHA** *appears beside her.)*

**TONIA**. 'Dearest Yurii... I pray you live to read this; it seems nowhere in Russia's safe for our kind anymore. We leave Moscow tonight, for Paris – Papa died peacefully in his sleep. Our son's been very strong through it all. You'd be proud of him. I met Lara Antipova. I wanted so much to hate her... but in the end, I think I understood...'

*(As* **TONIA** *sings,* **YURII** *continues reading aloud the letter she wrote.)*

| **TONIA.** | **YURII.** |
| --- | --- |
| WATCH THE MOON AND THINK OF ME. WATCH THE MOON I'LL WATCH IT, TOO. UNTIL THE DAY THAT YOU RETURN I'LL WATCH THE MOON AND THINK OF YOU... | She's the passionate flame a poet needs. How I wish I could have been that for you. Dearest Yurochka, my heart breaks when I think I may never see you again. But if you survive, do one thing for me; go outside on a clear night, the way we used to... |

*(***SASHA*** takes ***TONIA***'s hand, and they leave.)*

**YURII**. I have to get word to them.

**LARA**. They sealed the province; no more mail in or out. All we can do now is wait, and pray the soldiers pass us by.

**YURII**. Sit here and do nothing? That's madness.

**LARA**. It's Russia that's mad, Yurii.

**YURII**. I'm a fugitive. I deserted the Partisans. And now you're my accomplice. We'll both be sentenced to death.

**LARA**. Listen to me, my darling... all this time I didn't know if you were alive, and I thought back on everything, everything – how I married Pasha hoping to erase my past; how you married Tonia hoping for order and peace. But both of us were hungry for something we'd only ever find with each other. Right or wrong, whatever time is left us before the Red Army comes, we can be together, as it should have always been.

## [MUSIC NO. 21 - ON THE EDGE OF TIME]

I knew it the moment someone passed me the poem, scribbled on paper. When I began to read, I heard your voice so clearly.

WHEN YOU SPOKE YOU BROKE ME OPEN,
SET MY MIND AND BODY SOARING.
EV'RY WORD I STILL REMEMBER,
EV'RY WHISPER CARRIES THROUGH.

**YURII.**

IN YOUR EYES I SAW THE STARLIGHT
LIKE A BEACON NEVER DIMMING.
IN YOUR ARMS I WAS FORGIVEN,
LIFTED HIGHER, BORN ANEW...
YOU ARE ALWAYS THERE,
BEYOND THE DARK
LIGHTING MY EXISTENCE.
YOU, MY ANSWERED PRAYER,
MY MIDNIGHT SUN,
GLOWING IN THE DISTANCE.
DARING ME TO DREAM,
BLAZING FROM AFAR.
ONE STAR TO GUIDE ME THROUGH
AND LEAD ME HERE,
ON THE EDGE OF TIME WITH YOU.

**LARA.**

YOU SHOW ME A PLACE
WHERE HOPE IS REAL,
NOT A MERE ILLUSION.
ONE UNGUARDED SPACE
MY HEART CAN HEAL

FROM ITS MAD CONFUSION.
SHELTERED FROM THE STORM
IN YOUR WARM EMBRACE,
A GRACE I NEVER KNEW
I KNOW AT LAST
ON THE EDGE OF TIME WITH YOU.

**YURII.**

ALL THE PAIN, ALL THE YEARS,
OF SILENT DESPAIR.

**BOTH.**

ALL AT ONCE DISAPPEAR
LIKE MIST IN THE AIR,
LIKE MIST IN THE AIR!

*(She takes his hand, leading him to bed.)*

LET ME SHARE UNHURRIED DAYS
WHAT DAYS ARE LEFT
IN YOUR LOVE'S PROTECTION.

**YURII.**

HOLD YOU IN MY ARMS
SO I CAN FEEL
GOD IN HIS PERFECTION.

| **YURII.** | **LARA.** |
|---|---|
| THIS IS WHY I LIVE. | WHY I LIVE. |
| THIS IS KNOW IS REAL. | ONLY THIS IS REAL. |

**BOTH.**

TO FEEL THE WAY I DO, FOREVER FREE.

**YURII.**

FOREVER TRUE.

**BOTH.**

ON THE EDGE OF TIME WITH YOU.

*(They kiss tenderly. The lights dim.)*

## Scene 2–12: Military Hearing

**[MUSIC NO. 21A – MILITARY HEARING]**

(**STRELNIKOV** *stands guarded by two officers of the People. A* **SECRETARY** *for the People's Tribunal reads.*)

**SECRETARY.** Commander Strelnikov, the People's Tribunal finds you guilty of the crime of individualism and treason against the Worker's Revolutionary Party, whom you once claimed to support. Do you have anything to say in your defense?

(**STRELNIKOV** *is silent.*)

Your sentence is death. Take him away.

(*An eerie wolf howl. Lights dim. We are in...*)

## Scene 2–13: Abandoned Room in Kruger Mansion 'Ice Palace'

(**LARA** *and* **YURII** *awake. Time has passed. Another unearthly howl outside.*)

**LARA**. The wolves aren't afraid of us. They're moving closer.

**KOMAROVSKY**. Luckily they haven't learned to open doors yet.

> (**VIKTOR**, *wrapped in a once-luxurious, now frayed fur coat, rises slowly from an easy chair.*)

You were asleep when I arrived. I hated to disturb you. I had a chair like this in Moscow. Ideal for short naps.

**LARA**. How did you find us?

**KOMAROVSKY**. Everyone knows. You've been hiding in this old mansion for weeks.

**YURII**. What do you want?

**KOMAROVSKY**. Allow me to do you both a favor.

**LARA**. We want nothing from you, Viktor Ippolitovich.

**KOMAROVSKY**. The Red Army will come for you any day. I've secured a private railway carriage east to the sea. From there we'll find passage to Japan, Paris, wherever you like.

**YURII**. And in return?

**KOMAROVSKY**. (*To* **YURII**, *urgently.*) A word in private, Zhivago?

> (**YURII** *beckons* **LARA**. *Reluctantly, she leaves them alone.*)

# [MUSIC NO. 21B – KOMAROVSKY RETURNS]

**YURII.** I know about the two of you.

**KOMAROVSKY.** Spare me the sentimental scenes. There's only one reason you're alive, and it's gone now.

**YURII.** What, you?

**KOMAROVSKY.** Pasha Antipov. Lara's husband; you'd know him as –

**YURII.** Strelnikov, yes.

**KOMAROVSKY.** And did you know he dreamed of winning her back one day? He never stopped loving her. And he knew if you came to harm, Lara would never forgive him. But now he's dead.

**YURII.** Strelnikov?

**KOMAROVSKY.** Of course. The battle's won. It's time for the politicians; Purists like Strelnikov frighten them. You have no protector left on earth – except me. Swallow your pride and accept my help.

**YURII.** *(Realizing.)* You're still in love with her.

**KOMAROVSKY.** *(His silence speaks volumes.)* She won't leave here without you.

**YURII.** I can't travel. There's a reward for my capture.

**KOMAROVSKY.** I can get us out of the country. I've new identities for all *three of us*; passports, travel permits, safe passage documents, everything official –

**YURII.** I'm a wanted man, Komarovsky. They'd hang us all on the spot if I were identified. But the two of you without me stand a chance.

**KOMAROVSKY.** She'd rather stay here with you and die by your side.

**YURII**. *(Decides, calculating.)* Tell her... tell her I'll join you
further down the rail line, beyond Yuriatin.

**KOMAROVSKY**. She'd never believe *me*. But she'll always
believe you.

**YURII**. *(Thinking it through.)* Wait outside. I'll talk to her.
I'll find a way.

**KOMAROVSKY**. *(Not entirely persuaded.)* We should start
at least an hour before daylight. I'll be in the stables.

> *(**KOMAROVSKY** leaves. The slamming door
> brings **LARA** back.)*

**YURII**. He's outside. He's waiting.

**LARA**. What did you promise him?

**YURII**. He's our only hope, Lara. Go with him.

**LARA**. *(Adamant.)* <u>Both</u> of us.

> *(A slight hesitation, then he brings her coat:)*

**YURII**. Yes, of course. I'll pack my papers and join you
beyond Yuriatin. Tomorrow at the latest. We'll travel
east together, all three of us.

## [MUSIC NO. 21C – NOW (REPRISE)]

**LARA**. Please don't ask me to be alone with him.

**YURII**. Only until the next stop on the line. I'll join you
there when you're out of danger.

**LARA**. Promise you'll meet us. Promise on our love.

**YURII**. *(After the briefest moment.)* You know I'd never let
you out of my sight if I wasn't sure we'd be together
soon; without you my life has no meaning.

**LARA**. Oh, Yurochka, tell me you mean it?

**YURII**. *(Lying.)* Have I ever lied to you?

> *(A moment passes while things sink in.)*

These last few weeks with you, they're just the beginning.

**LARA**. *(Struggling with this.)* I was saving this 'til I was sure, but you should know; making love here, I felt a change inside. It might mean nothing at all... or there may be someone new in our lives...

**YURII**. *(Nodding.)* Hurry.

> *(They kiss, passionate, a moment to last a lifetime. She rushes out. When **LARA** leaves, **YURII***'s self-control cracks.)*

NOW, I NEED TO LET YOU LIVE
AND HOPE THAT YOU FORGIVE
WHAT I HAVE DONE.
BE STRONG AND PURE
THROUGH ALL YOU MUST ENDURE.
LET NOTHING DIM
THE BRIGHTNESS OF YOUR SUN.
I CAN SEE YOU SOARING
LIKE A BIRD IN FLIGHT,
AND I PRAY TO GOD
WHAT I DID WAS RIGHT.

> *(He spots the vodka bottle, and drinks. He then turns towards his desk, and crosses to it. He sits, pulls out loose paper and a pen from the drawer.)*

Now...as shadows fall, you...you the night. Softly surround me. Stars become your eyes. The wind your voice...

> *(He begins to write. As he does, his poem is projected behind him in handwritten Russian Cyrillic, the full height of the stage. As the light darkens, at last only the words in white are visible through the darkness. Time passes. **YURII** falls into a deep sleep.)*

## Scene 2-13B: The Ice Palace in the Morning Light

*(A distant wolf howls. Morning streams in revealing a **MAN** in a tattered uniform, pistol drawn, breaking into the ice palace. He looks wild, dangerous. Seeing the vodka bottle, he snatches it and drinks deeply, then slams the bottle down. **YURII** starts, gazing around bleary-eyed.)*

**STRELNIKOV**. Where is she?

**YURII**. Strelnikov? I thought you were –

**STRELNIKOV**. Everyone does. I'm a cat; nine lives. I came to say goodbye to Lara.

**YURII**. She's gone.

**STRELNIKOV**. Where?

**YURII**. Japan? Paris? Who knows.

**STRELNIKOV**. *(Eerie detachment.)* In that case, I'll never see her again.

> *(He raises bottle in a bitter toast.)*

To those we'll never see again.

> *(He chugs, then offers the bottle to **YURII**.)*

Drink with me.

> *(**YURII** takes the bottle and drinks from it.)*

I'm her husband.

**YURII**. I know.

**STRELNIKOV**. *(Grins.)* And you're her lover. But she's gone now. And the two of us have unfinished business. How would you describe my wife, Y.A Zhivago.

> *(Feverish.)*

Would you call her a woman of passionate appetites?

**YURII**. I'd rather not talk about her.

**STRELNIKOV**. *(With a sneer.)* Really?

> *(He picks up the poem on the table that* **YURII** *has been writing.)*

Isn't this talk?! Of course not, it's 'poetry.' But about her, am I right? You can't help yourself, it's what she does to a man.

> *(He crumples the poem, throws it on the floor.)*

**YURII**. What are your plans?

**STRELNIKOV**. First, I'll finish this vodka. In the company of my wife's lover. Whose life I once spared. Then, I'll dream about a young man I knew: a child obsessed with a woman, who threw away his life to rid the world of everything that corrupted her.

**YURII**. She was never corrupt. The wrong she did never touched her heart.

**STRELNIKOV**. *(Waving his gun, unaware.)* Don't lecture me about my wife. I gave my life to revenge her shame. What did you do for her, except write poems.

**YURII**. I loved her.

**STRELNIKOV**. *(Watches him carefully.)* Love! Yes... to love.

> *(Drinks, then offers.)*

Have some, it's your bottle. Tell me, poet, what's it like for love to be enough?

**YURII**. You loved the Revolution? Wasn't that 'enough?'

**STRELNIKOV**. *(After a moment.)* Everything betrays us in the end.

**YURII**. Everything fills us with life if we let it.

**STRELNIKOV**.  *(A rueful laugh.)* And here we are; an aristocrat and a railway worker's son. The revolution was a success. It made us equals after all: two enemies of the state, sick with love for the same woman.

> *(**STRELNIKOV** kicks the wadded poem on the floor, contemptuously.)*

**YURII**. Would you put that back on the table please?

### [MUSIC NO. 21D – THE DEATH OF STRELNIKOV]

> *(**STRELNIKOV** smirks at **YURII**'s absurd concern for what amounts to nothing at all, but as he picks up the page, he can't resist reading the poem. He grows engrossed, in spite of himself. If we were closer, we'd see his eyes water.)*

**STRELNIKOV**.  *(Bewildered by his own feelings.)* This is Lara...

> *(Sets the poem on the table, turns to leave.)*

The villagers thought I was the devil. Wait till they see the Russian dreamers who take my place. I'll be remembered as a saint!!

> *(**STRELNIKOV** draws his revolver and leaves, a man without purpose. A cry outside.)*

LARA!!

> *(A gunshot. **YURII** approaches the door, **STRELNIKOV** lies gun in hand, head in a pool of blood. **YURII** stares at the body.)*

### [MUSIC NO. 21E – BLOOD ON THE SNOW (REPRISE)]

*(The Red Flag of Communist Russia lowers behind. Russian* **BUREAUCRATS***, finally mighty in their drab triumph, march across stage as the ice palace vanishes, and* **YURII** *stands aside watching, a witness to the Soviet future.)*

*(They reprise the song of the soldiers on the battlefield, now become a propagandistic anthem.)*

## Scene 2–14: The Bureaucracy

**BUREAUCRATS.**
>BLOOD ON THE SNOW,
>THE RED FLAG ARISING,
>BATHED IN THE GLEAM
>OF A NEW WORLD REGIME.
>FORWARD MARCH TO THE DRUM,
>THE TRUMPETS OF THUNDER.
>SHACKLES ASUNDER,
>FREE FOR A THOUSAND YEARS TO COME!

## Scene 2-15: Moscow Several Years Later – A Cemetery

### Projection Title: MOSCOW - WINTER 1930

*(When the* **BUREAUCRATS** *exit,* **STRELNIKOV***'s body is gone.)*

*(***LARA** *and a girl,* **KATARINA***, stand by a grave together with a* **PRIEST** *– and no one else. It is deserted but for the three of them.)*

**PRIEST.** Today, we mourn the passing of a gentle spirit, who lived his final years among the poor of Moscow, as a doctor, until his heart gave out. But in secret, he wrote verse. His work, banned by the state – as our church is banned – won a following so passionate and wide the authorities never dared harm him, though he could never travel, forced to live as a captive of the state. His work, however, travelled freely from hand to hand, and finally around the world, until he is now hailed as the great Russian poet of the century. His inspiration, the woman who haunts every line he wrote, is still a mystery, but she has become for many a symbol of the Russian spirit: patient, unyielding, and irresistibly beautiful. Go with God, Yurii Andreyevich Zhivago.

*(The* **PRIEST** *exits, leaving* **LARA** *and* **KATARINA** *alone at the graveside.)*

**KATARINA.** Why is no one else here, mama?

**LARA.** They're afraid, darling. Yurochka, my dearest, dearest – this is our daughter, Katarina. Her voice is so like yours when she speaks. In Paris children study your poems in school. Imagine! It's strange to hear our private moments spoken in public. Sometimes I'm embarrassed. Sometimes I'm proud. Sometimes for a moment I see myself through your eyes and feel you so close to me.

*(She brushes tears from her eyes.)*

Recite the poem for your father, darling. Let him hear his daughter's voice.

## [MUSIC NO. 22 – FINALE ACT II]

*(**KATARINA** reads from the book of poems.)*

**KATARINA.**  Now, as shadows fall, you are the night.
Softly you surround me.
Stars become your eyes,
The wind your voice,
Whispering around me ...
RISING IN THE GLOW
OF THE CANDLE'S GLEAM.

**LARA & KATARINA.**
ONE DREAM, FOREVER NEW.
MY LIFE IS HERE
ON THE EDGE OF TIME WITH YOU.

**LARA.**
PURE AS SUMMER RAIN.
THE AUTUMN SUN,
DANCING ON THE RIVER.
FROST UPON THE PLAIN.
THE SEEDS OF SPRING
WAKING WITH A SHIVER.

*(A light snow begins to fall.)*

| **TONIA.** | **ENSEMBLE.** |
|---|---|
| GROVES OF SILVER BIRCH | AH |
| AGELESS AND SERENE | AH |
| GROW GREEN BENEATH | |
| THE BLUE | |

**TONIA.**                    **ENSEMBLE.**

AS SEASONS PASS
ON THE EDGE OF TIME
   WITH YOU.

*(More* **MOURNERS** *arrive, each checking that they weren't followed. As the scene unfolds they remove concealed books of* **YURII***'s poetry as they sing.)*

*(***RED GUARDS** *who have found their way to this clandestine gathering, also take out their copies of* **YURII***'s verse.)*

**ENSEMBLE.**          **TWO SOPRANOS & TWO TENORS.**

YOU, THE SEA. I, THE SHORE.    OOH
ETERNAL, WE BLEND.          **TWO TENORS & TWO BARITONES.**

MOVING ON EVERMORE,      AHH

**ALL.**

A LINE WITHOUT END.
A LINE WITHOUT END...!
I ASCEND BEYOND THE PALE,
ABOVE THE STORM
BREATHING IN YOUR SPIRIT.
THOUGH MY HEART IS FRAIL,
AND DEATH WILL COME,
I NO LONGER FEAR IT.
NATIONS RISE AND FALL
TYRANTS COME AND GO...

*(***YURII** *appears.)*

**YURII.**

I KNOW WHEN LIFE IS THROUGH,
MY LOVE WILL LIVE
IN A RAY OF LIGHT...

**LARA.**

IN A DISTANT CHIME...

**YURII & LARA.**

ON THE EDGE OF TIME WITH YOU.

*(Distant chimes sound as the snow falls.)*

## End of Play

**[MUSIC NO. 23 – BOWS]**

**[MUSIC NO. 24 – EXIT MUSIC]**

www.ingramcontent.com/pod-product-compliance
Lightning Source LLC
Chambersburg PA
CBHW071924130726
47909CB00014B/2573